THE YELLOW SERPENT

Tales, Musings & Memories

by

D. Gemcats Purcell
&
Catherine G. Purcell

PROLOGUE:

Gemma is a ten-year-old young lady who lives with her mother
and an older sister in a poor country village on the island nation
of Camerhogne. They are a poor family with only the very faded
patina of being middle class. She is about to transition from
Primary school to High School and she along with her fellow
classmates, are filled with dread about the transition. For her age
she is very observant and is keen to avoid impact of all the
negative forces that are growing in her life. She is keenly aware
of how those forces often truncates young girls progress toward a
healthy productive adult life. Her only mentor really is Dr.
Benny her Godfather, with her real father, an alcoholic being
already dead. Contending with the scary energy-sapping fairy
tales that abound in her village society, her own childhood
insecurities, a dangerous predatory environment for young girls,
as well as the often poor teaching resources that were available,
are a major part of the challenges she finds herself having to
negotiate.

CREDITS:

To my wife Catherine co-author and upon whose life this book is
generally patterned though not amounting to a full
autobiography. It is therefore ultimately a book of fiction. Any
resemblance to known places and actual people in Camerhogne
is purely accidental or unintended therefore. All place names in

Camerhogne are fictional and are not intended to reference actual locations.
We must mention our supporters who were willing to take our calls and answer questions: Nurse Cynthia Telesford, Dr. Louis Telesford, Professor Kester Peters and Mum Bernadette Frederick and Brother Rodney Frederick our major proof readers.

ISBN: 978-1-7372497-5-7

CHAPTERS:

Chapter 1 - Meet the serpent

It had been a disturbing night with fitful sleep. It was now just past the second crowing of the cock. Gemma's eyes cracked open reluctantly and at first, she couldn't believe what she was seeing. What was that yellow fruit hanging in the rafters over her bed she sleepily thought to herself; it was such a very odd-looking fruit indeed. She thought as she slowly began to focus that there might be some slight movement of the fruit but of course it was still too dark to be sure. Dawn was just creeping in, barely making its presence felt with only the faintest lightening of the sky reaching through the open rafters to glint off the underside of the metal galvanized roof.

It was that vague movement that finally snapped her wide awake, now staring fixedly. There shouldn't be any fruit hanging from the roof. Every sense in her body, every muscle was tense, straining, trying to discern her environment. She felt the soft breathing of her mom laying no more than a foot away, the warm moistness of her back laying against her rough sheet and something sticky round and firm between her elbow and the side of her rib cage. Another galba seed dropped off by the bats she rapidly concluded. There wasn't a night that went by without them waking up to the dubious joy of half-eaten seeds being dropped onto them by bats that flew in through the wide-open rafters. There was a large enough gap between the walls of their tiny wooden house and the underside of the galvanized roof with its attached wooden rafters. Perched upside down with their claws clamped to those rafters they ate whatever fruits they'd carried in with them, before dispensing the remnants, often skins and seeds directly below them. The variety of seeds and fruit remnants dropped were enormous, from galba to penny piece, sapodillas, almonds, sea wet, water melon, bouyee, hog plums, water lemons, resulting in constantly soiled bedsheets and very 'icky' things sleeping with them, bat excrement included.

The cock had just crowed a second time as it does every morning at around five-thirty. It's first time to crow is usually at four in the morning. The night had been a disturbed one for her. She had even heard the whine of Cokette's big board bus 'Bella Marie' as it made a stop two hundred feet away where he would have been picking up Mrs. Goldie with her tons of produce and provisions going to set up her stall in the market in the capital city of Fredericktown. That happens at four-fifteen in the am. Although she had done her homework early by seven that night, brushed her teeth with a cup of water, done her business into the 'utensil' and stored it safely under the bed and was covered head to toe under her sheet by eight o'clock, sleep took several tawdry hours to come. At least that's how it felt. So, when the cock crowed on the cocoa tree a few feet away from her window the first time, she fretted with frustration. Mostly if she was woken up by the crowing, she'd remember later in the morning that it happened, as she would almost instantly have fallen back to sleep. This night and this particular morning were not at all like that. It felt like sleep had been a battle and she still was tired. When she was harshly roused by the second crowing, she then realized that she had to have slipped back blissfully into a brief nap in the interim though by no means did she feel rested. Now normally she could count on another hour or so of sleep, but there was no going back this time.

It was then that she had first noticed the unwelcome sight above her bed. She was uneasy now having recognized what was above her bed, above her own skinny stretched out legs. It was a serpent, coiled from the wooden rafters, twisted upon itself like a large fruit, just like the one she had battled in her dream. It had likely already eaten its bat or gecko 'wood slave' but she couldn't yet see its telltale bulge clearly. The dawn was racing into the rafters though and she thought or maybe imagined seeing those baleful reddish unblinking eyes staring fixedly at her.

Her initial inclination was to bump her mom with her elbow, but instead she froze, just hoping it would simply go away. Her much older sister was sleeping on her own narrow built-in bed with her rather well-worn mattress on it jammed up against the wall in the adjacent bedroom. Serpents hanging from the rafters happened every few weeks it felt to Gemma, but rarely over their bed! Bats were there every night with the resulting detritus and resulted in the constant work of joining their neighbors to do the washing of those big bedsheets on the river stones most Saturday mornings. This was part of their village and neighborhood ritual here in Zion. However, after squeezing her eyes for about a full minute tightly as if to will the serpent away, she reluctantly opened them to behold the same sight. She could not take her eyes off the beast. She had begun, at least to 'inch' that half eaten fleshy seed away from her by reaching over with her right hand and pushing it in her mom's direction under her slightly elevated left arm. It took a bit of effort as she was in a slight depression on the soft mattress and it was pushing a slippery seed uphill. She felt better just getting it away from her. It felt like her night was one nonstop series of skirmishes, none of which had been pleasant. At least she had school and her few friends to look forward to come nine o'clock that morning.

Yes, most of Gemma's nights were tawdry, listless affairs filled with dreams and nightmares which she absolutely dreaded. What was sad and even more scary was that her nights were often filled with unpleasant events even before she fell asleep. There were the otherworldly screams of fighting or maybe mating feral cats which seemed to love the cleared areas in her mom's yard to carryon. Since her mother's decrepit house had rotten wooden floorboards and walls, there were lots of holes for entry and egress of insects and small animals. The so-called front door could simply be pushed open with minimal force by any intruder and just to give a semblance of resistance, any heavy object such as a table or chair was usually placed behind it. Any willing thief or worse could simply push his or her hand through a hole in the front door itself and push aside that bench or whatever other object was placed there and then the door would open easily. Certainly, a shoulder with body weight behind it could gain entrance not just through the front door, likely through any wall of the house. How many times have cats not jumped over Gemma's chest in mid sleep all the while squealing and snarling, waking her up from deep sleep! At times, it felt like she lived in a wild cat playhouse. Some nights were exceedingly scary indeed in the Crawford household.

Gemma noticed a change in her mom's breathing and while still looking at the serpent fixedly, she gently canted her head toward her and said, " Mom mom!" It was said with a tone of alarm and her mother cued into that, instantly awake. She asked, "What's wrong Gemma?"

Gemma said, "Mom there is a serpent hanging right over the bed, above us!" She felt her mom's weight shift on the bed as she turned her head to look up and then heard her mom's exclamation, "Oh my gosh, it's right directly above us!" With that she felt her mom scooting not so gently off the bed saying, "Move child, move out of there, if that thing falls, it will land on top of you." Gemma's limbs, previously frozen in fear, loosened suddenly with her mother's exhortation and she quickly shimmied off the bed dragging her covering sheet with her. Mom and daughter were now standing at the foot of the bed. Gemma's sister Mavis had heard the commotion and was out of her tiny bedroom even before them. Gemma suddenly saw a coconut fiber broom gripped in defensive fashion in the hand of her mom. It was a mystery to Gemma how brooms could so quickly appear in her mother's hands. A strange dog comes into the yard and is about to attack our own little pup tied under the house to a supporting post, and the broom would appear. If some religious nut came by the house to give out church tracts, the broom appeared threateningly waving accompanied with shouts of, "Take your religion, get out of here and don't ever let me see you back in this yard or you will get a utensil full of stale pee." This was no idle threat. Gemma could vouch for mom G, having seen her actually carry out that threat. Mom G was pushing her wide hips against the side of Gemma's right chest and shoulder to get her to sidle away from the bedroom into the cramped little space they called the living dining room. Mom and her brooms have a long-lasting loving relationship, Gemma had long ago realized, particularly after having it lashed brusquely against her own bum once or twice.

The dawn had matured to the point that now the line of water droplets hanging from the troughs of the wavy exposed galvanized metal roofing, having condensed there with the cool overnight temperatures, were now clearly visible. They resembled what Gemma thought a row of cloudy diamonds would look like; gems that she giggled privately she may never really see. Of course, mom G had a few cheap pearl necklaces in her private drawer that rarely ever saw the light of day. Those prized trinkets would only emerge in full display around mom G's neck accompanied by her famous broaches on very special occasions like a rare family portrait event that had only happened once she was aware of, or a special wedding of a close friend or family member maybe. Maybe she would deem to wear a broach on her chest for special church celebrations or funerals. Gemma also knew that should those drops, for whatever reason, decide to take leave of the galvanized roof and land on the bedsheets or other items of clothing, brown rust stains would be their lasting gift. That was why all 'good' clothing had to be covered up inside of plastic garment bags. There weren't any actual built-in cupboards for storing clothing like up at Mr. Renwick's. Their home was too tiny and dingy for that.

Before too long, mom had thrown open two of the wooden windows allowing more light into the otherwise darkened house which was bereft of electric lights. There was no electricity in their tiny wooden home and it was rapidly becoming too bright anyway to justify lighting a candle or engaging the sole kerosene lantern. With a rumble, the wooden bench that had been jammed against the otherwise truly unbolted front door was pulled back by Mavis her much taller and older adult sister who was almost eighteen, already finished with high school and who already was holding down a job. The clack and rattle of the very rickety wooden door frame with its few panes of easily removable glass slats seemed loud as it was pulled back. Mom G was out in a flash just behind Mavis, after she had pulled on her outside flip flops. She returned with the cocoa knife that had been leaning against the one soursop tree in their yard. This hand sized, black metal axe shaped blade with a side projection resembling a human thumb, was mounted on a fifteen-foot-long rod of bamboo. Gemma quickly stepped aside, as the knife was thrust through the open door by mom who was simultaneously lifting it up, so that it would slide in above the cloth curtained separation between the living dining room space and their bedroom area. The bedroom section had been divided into two mini- bedrooms with one larger than the other with a wooden board wall between them. This wooden separation was only as high as the curtain though. So in effect, everyone everywhere in the whole house looked up to see the same rafters and the under-surface of the galvanized roof.

She was aiming straight at the rafters where their dear serpent rested twirled around on itself. Mavis was out on the grass, arms crossed about her chest over her ragged off-white nightie. It seemed to sense danger approaching because there was a sudden emergence of its head from among its coils and with its beady reddish unblinking eyes looking at them, began to flick its forked tongue quickly back and forth. Things were getting exciting, really more like scary now, to be honest. There was an elastic cable strung from wall to wall, the width of the house which basically was about twenty feet wide and taller than mom G's head. On that long cable was hung four long sheets looped through it forming a curtain. This afforded a good amount of separation between the two areas of the house so that a visitor walking into the living dining area could not immediately see into the either of the two small bedroom areas.

So, knowing that her mom wanted and indeed needed the curtains moved, Gemma stepped back toward the bedroom area and dragged the sheets that acted as curtains aside toward each wall, thus opening up the two ordinarily separate spaces to each other. The house was about thirty feet long and there was a tiny kitchen out pouched area off the living dining area with a small sink and a meager four-foot wooden countertop space adjacent, with just enough floor width to allow one person at a time to step in there. Opposite the sink, was a tiny shelf on which sat a flat cooktop run by kerosene for indoor cooking on wet rainy days only. Normally all cooking took place outside on the 'charcoal pot' or a few feet away also outdoors on a wood burning fireside, where the pot would be set and balanced on three to four stones. Anyway, now mom G with the additional visual clearance now available, began to advance her cocoa knife into the bedroom above the curtain line, progressively elevating her long rod with its blade aiming for the yellow now very active serpent. Gemma's heart was pounding now with excitement. As mom G advanced to do battle with the serpent, Gemma inched her way toward the front door past her mom, backing up slowly, eyes fixed on the serpent and the approaching cocoa knife. Her great fear was that the serpent might launch itself at the advancing blade with its attached rod. Her skin crawled in fear of that thing touching her, Lord forbid crawling and knotting itself around her. The very thought terrified her. Some of the boys in her class who had touched and even claimed to have played with them during carnival, had said that they were totally cold to the touch, like a dead person would be. She shivered again at the thought.

The serpent was now within striking distance of mom's blade and rod and it wasted no time. Mom wavered a little as she could feel the obvious impacts on her attacking implement. She regained her composure and commenced to prod the vicious yellow banded beady-eyed monster. Gemma's memories of her dreams surged back into her mind. This felt like deja vu to her and for several moments standing there, she became acutely dissociated, not being really sure if this was real or part of one of her dreams. She couldn't shake the cloying impression that she had met this very same yellow serpent before, even just last night, and on many previous nights too.

Gemma somehow snapped back into reality, maybe aided by the splinter on the edge of the weathered wooden door frame poking her painfully when she had inadvertently leaned her bony shoulder on it. Mom had skillfully taunted the creature into lengthening itself in its zeal to strike out at its tormenting knife and rod. With that mom had twirled the hooked thumb of the cocoa knife around its body spinning the bamboo around and around in her hands, enticing the animal to start coiling around the bamboo shaft. Slowly mom then retracted the rod and blade while continuing to twist and now she pulled and pulled while inching herself backwards toward the open doorway. The serpent was thus detached from the rafters reluctantly, coiled on the end of the rod which mom strained to keep elevated as she slowly continued her careful backup toward the wide-open door. Mavis by now had backed up into their joint mostly compacted gravel driveway shared with Mr. Renwick a good forty feet away from the front steps.

Gemma needed no encouragement to get out of the way. She turned around and with an alarmed low frightened shriek sped down the three rickety steps to the ground barefooted. Mom followed still backing up straining with the heavy snake coiled into a ball on the end of the bamboo rod. The cocoa knife part of the rod was enveloped by the coils of the creature but its head was up, watchful, forked tongue darting in and out. Gemma scrambled around towards the back of the house pebbles poking the bare soles of her feet, frantically trying to put distance between herself and that rod with its yellow coils. Mom was now on the grass and huffing to keep the now very heavy rod lifted up as it now emerged through the doorway.

Finally, the serpent was out of the house, Gemma thought with relief. If it were later in the day, mom would have carried the rod out the two hundred fifty feet to the main road where inevitably there would be passing young men of the neighborhood who would take it from her to get rid of it. Now, it was too early in the morning for that and mom was not really appropriately dressed anyway, having come straight out of bed dressed in a simple partly torn nightgown, hair undone. So, she instead went down the grassy, only partially cleared pathway leading to the garden, thence a good two hundred feet to the edge of the stream. There she flung the rod violently, with seeming practiced ease in a semicircular manner above her head, starting with the rod behind her violently toward her front. The poor serpent was catapulted from the end of the rod way across the stream into the bushes on the far side, a good forty feet at least.

There was only a vague twitch of the tall grasses to mark the serpent's uncontrolled landing. This was close to the huge haunted sand box tree with its serpentine huge roots that supported a great chunk of the river bank in that locale. Its roots invaded their way into the river water forming dark deep mysterious pools in the area. People warned children to avoid that area for fear of the roots grabbing and drowning them. The seeds of the tree made all kinds of eerie noises when they fell, since they exploded spraying seeds if they impacted a hard object like a branch, on the way down. The resultant mini-explosions sounded like fire crackers going off day and night. That only served to confirm that truly it's base and that portion of the river was the meeting place of the devil, jumbies, lajabless and obeah people. Gemma could still smell the scent of the serpent lingering on the rod, as her mom had walked past. Gemma had been sure to stay within sight of the slinging operation, but far enough behind so that should the serpent detach from the rod prematurely when mom had swung the rod sideways and a bit behind her to gather momentum, it would not land near her. Mom said to no one in particular, "Don't you come back in my house serpent!" Shaking her head as we walked back up the pathway, she murmured, "I bet it will be back. I needed to get it further away from the house. It had a bulge in its belly, so it must have just eaten. It will remember where it got its food - in our rafters! I really should have killed the bugger. It was a big heavy one."

Gemma didn't say anything. She was hoping and praying that the serpent would find better hunting grounds elsewhere, other than over her bed!

Christmas had not long passed. It was still early January and it was cold. Well, it was cold by the standards of the Caribbean island of Camerhogne in January. Despite the expected cold water, it was totally an understood thing that both mom G and Gemma hurriedly went to the outdoor pipe stand to get their legs cleaned off. This was where they showered too; their privacy was somewhat protected from prying eyes on three sides, by tall strips of makeshift galvanized roofing sheets. They had been outside walking in the yard. That was cause to wash off one's feet in and of itself! Plus, they had been down to the river a short maybe hundred and fifty feet away with dew dampened wet cool grass touching their legs and feet. Tons of grass seeds and other detritus were likely tarring their legs. Gemma could feel the stuff sticking uncomfortably to her legs. Then they quickly made their way back inside, hopping as much as possible on the strategically placed stones between the grass patches growing in the yard. Mom G jokingly said, "We really ought to be ashamed of ourselves talking about being cold! Can you imagine your poor brother Damian and his wife Wren who told us two days ago that they were in the deep freezer having to use poles to probe the snowbanks to find where their car was, after the snowplows had passed on their street in Brooklyn!" Gemma shuddered at the thought, sort of anyway, because the thought of snow actually excited her. She just could not truly imagine what it would be like...

She tried to imagine what it would be like to touch it, to walk in it, and having seen a few rare videos-ski in it! She mused to herself, "Do you ski on it or in it?" Anyway, back to the matters at hand; hop up the stairs, quickly pull the door shut and after peering at the rafters again to make sure that snake's mate had not come looking for it, she ventured into the bedroom to get some more clothes on. A quick towel rub down to dry off got first attention. After all, she felt even more chilled after the dose of cold mountain water o her legs. By nine o'clock with the sun up over the hills it would be warm. The dew on the grass would have burnt off and the galvanized roofing would be giving its first crinkling sounds as it heated up, drying the collected drops of water now hanging suspended over their heads. As they had made their way back in, they noticed there were wet spots outlining the shape of the house all along the grass and stones where condensation from the roof both topside and underside had coalesced and dripped. Their dog Cereal who had been barking loudly in sympathy with their distress over the serpent even lunging at it when mom G had emerged with it coiled on the end of the cocoa knife got a pat on his head, as they had been hopping by from stone to stone after their ablutions. He always eagerly sought out their touch, straining at his leash attached to one of the house posts, hoping to get inside. His bed was a few old wadded crocus bags over a few scraps of old discarded wooden planks safely away from the rain under the house, but positioned so he could see the comings and goings around the house and yard. He had overlook status relative to a few other neighbors' yards too, just because mom G's house was on the side of a little hillock. Consequently, there was barking sometimes all night long triggered by events such as visitations to the single mom who lived across the street within sight of our house though not an immediate neighbor. God forbid, the gossip said too that there were visitations to her couple of her teenage daughters too! Rumor had it that various suitors had been observed climbing up and out of windows day and night.

Gemma would tell you that she had seen things happen all around her, that would make the pure of mind faint. So although she was only ten plus years old, having recently sat for and successfully passed her high school entrance exam, she would tell you that between her voracious reading and the things that she had beholden with her own eyes and ears, she was far far older! No, it wasn't just the periodic orgy of dogs mating for days pulling each other's insides out around tree trunks. It was also the parade of loose young girls her age or just a tad bit older who walked right past her mom's house going up the hill to visit the well to do Mr. Renwick's big house! It was witnessing the periodic, every few days fights between Mr. Branson, when he apparently came home 'drunk as a fish' and his wife Jenny. Somehow those 'fights' seemed to spill out from their bedroom onto the back porch. With his wife screaming what sounded like bloody murder to her ears, while saying, "more, more" and mom

G hurrying her from the yard where she would have been playing, into the supposed sanctuary of their bedroom and closing the doors and windows while telling Gemma, "Don't look!" That admonishment only served to entice Gemma to surreptitiously peep between the many spaces in the half-rotted walls of their house to get a glimpse. She had had a thorough 'schooling' in the saucy and grungy aspects of life over many years when she was even younger of course. Nowadays her mom would still dutifully admonish her to not look, but that would be totally and openly ignored by Gemma. That was no fighting, no fighting at all, she had long ago laughingly concluded. He would come home drunk and she would be waiting. The 'fighting' was simply a preamble to the theater like performance that would begin soon after. Who needed television? In fact, truth be told, one day she had had to return home a bit earlier than usual, only to catch her own darling mom in the act of heavy breathing plus goodness knows what else, with a gentleman who seemed to occasionally visit her to say 'hello'. Gemma's own dad had been a fall-down drunk too and had been transferred to heaven a mere three years ago. Those three years to her seemed like an eternity. Even when he too was alive, she had visited him at his place of business only to observe young ladies being extremely friendly with him. So, this carousing was a thing, a really big common thing all over. Pregnant young ladies too were a thing; they were all around, everywhere one went, oh dear.

Chapter 2 - Between dark and dawn.

Gemma being friendly with her Godmother the wife of Mr. Renwick, would actually spend quite a lot of her free time at their residence and therefore learned a lot of what dirty old men's tricks involved. She had even tried to warn some of those poor underage girls not to come up there, but to no avail. They likely had long ago been induced with his gifts to party away their virginities to him and his lecherous friends, likely including her Dr. Benny too. Gemma had long ago graduated into a very well-spoken but extremely knowledgeable youngster well able to stand up to the likes of Mr. Renwick, much to the delight of his sickly wife who obviously knew all about his evil undertakings. Gemma's 'tongue' certainly was well respected by him. After he had attempted to make his play on her, she had thoroughly tongue lashed him, as they say, 'up and down' letting him know that he would never get a piece of her and that she would sleep with all the miscreants in her village before she would consider having a 'dirty old geezer like him touch her.' It wasn't just that she said those words to him, but that she shouted it out, so that all the neighbors could hear. He had resorted to begging her to stop and bargaining with her to at least be quieter about it. Of course, the whole village knew him and there was braying laughter coming from a few nearby yards in response. Shouts of "dirty old man, leave the little child alone. She gave you good, just what you deserve," filled the air. Of course, his own wife who was mostly room bound terribly sick with a weak heart and badly swollen legs heard her and even egged Gemma on. "Don't let nasty old men take advantage of you child. I'm so proud of you Gemma. So good to see you stand up for yourself Darling."

One of his so-called best buddies was medical doctor Dr. Benny who was also her Godfather, believe it or not. So although he was a frequent visitor and likely participant in some of the games on the hill, Dr. Benny actually took a strong seemingly wholesome interest in Gemma. Gemma after all lived just a little lower down the hill from Mr. Renwick along his driveway essentially and Dr. Benny would stop to tell her to come join him up the hill whenever he was passing by. In addition, Mrs. Renwick was quite ill and they were her closest neighbor, so an old fashioned windup telephone had been strung between the two houses. That was yet another way for help to be summoned by Mrs. Renwick and yet another way for Dr. Benny to officially request Gemma's presence too! They had spent hours discussing books from Mr. Renwick's library as well as current national and world events. Mr. Renwick actually was considered one of Camerhogne's rich and among other things had an expansive library, mostly to impress the who and who that would often visit him and his wife. Gemma had never seen Mr. Renwick read and even early on, learned not to ask him questions about his own books as he never seemed to know the answers anyway.

Dr. Benny definitely had a very soft spot for Gemma and was clearly impressed by her sharp intellect and worldly knowledge. He quite explicitly answered and even explained answers to any questions about 'anatomy and body function' to Gemma whenever she asked. So, although her mother had said perfunctorily to her, "don't let boys touch you" as the totality of her sex education, Gemma by the age of ten had no more questions to ask that had not yet been answered. Her 'Mills and Boone' simplified love story books were still read and enjoyed, but this business of the clueless damsel swooning just about the time she met the tall dark and handsome rich dude was totally cliche and even silly to her already. She was schooled by her voracious reading, the reality of her village and Dr. Benny. Dr. Benny had appointed himself her protector too and he rather mischievously would come to her aid when it was not needed and when he knew he would cause her maximum embarrassment. He would be driving by her school going from one of his doctor's offices to another while she was on break and if per chance, he found Gemma among friends chatting with even one boy close by, he would stop, call over loudly to her with admonishments to keep away from such scurrilous members of the human race with the widest of grins on his face. Gemma would be teased for days by her compatriots and he would drive on quite happily. Her Godfather though a consummate prankster that way, as far as Gemma was concerned he was far more of a true father figure to her, she grudgingly had to admit, than her own constantly drunk father had been before the rum killed him.

Yet she really was still a child. Back in the house with her legs toweled dry now and away from the cold breeze outside and now covered up with one of her mom's thicker warmer long old dresses, she slid back into bed and covered herself up with a cleaner sheet. The messy seed dropping stained sheet, was relegated to the dirty clothes basket. Mom had given her a little hug and was already shuffling about in the kitchen area, no doubt getting ready for the day's project. Mom was a seamstress and there was a mechanical foot operated singer sewing machine parked in one corner of the living dining area space with mounds of clothing, plus various multicolored ends of cloth all around it. A rack with completed and almost complete dresses hung off a hook on the wall to the right of the machine. When she had walked past the machine, the characteristic scent of the machine oil used as a lubricant for the machine wafted welcomingly into her nostrils. Gemma again scanned the underside of the roof above her and found nothing troubling there, but still felt some residual unease from both an unrestful night's sleep plus the early morning events.

Her mom called out to her softly, "Gemma do you remember when we had just gotten into bed last night and we both heard a whooshing sound like a rope being twirled really fast in the air then what sounded like a branch falling on our metal roof and I had said then 'that's not good'. What I meant was that it likely was the sound of a snake flying off the big silk cotton tree up the hill above the house. They do that you know. Exactly what I feared would happen, did happen! It landed on our roof and crawled its way in. You noticed the big swelling in its body, well it probably gobbled up one of the bats that come in here to eat its fruit. I just didn't say it all out loud to alarm you, since it was near bedtime."

Gemma said simply, "Yes Mom. This has happened many times before, so I did think of that too, but I was hoping and praying that it wouldn't be. I forced myself off to sleep and I ended up dreaming of serpents. I even saw Mrs. Julia's face in one of my dreams. Her head was on the body of a serpent mom." All mom said to that was, "Did you say your prayers properly Gemma. You know little girls need to give a good long prayer. It helps you to sleep well and not see serpents!" Gemma protested meekly, "But I did mommy, I did." Gemma had realized that her mom did not want to listen to what she did not want to hear, like some of her novels said, 'ostriches burying their head in the sand.' Gemma thought, "It is what it is, one has got to know one's people and work with them in whatever way one can! That is who my mom is and she is the only one I'll ever have!" It was one of the realities that she and Dr. Benny had recently discussed actually learning about your closest family and friends, realizing that they, like you, aren't perfect.

Mom G could be heard moving about a few feet from her, though hidden behind the large cloth curtain now once again drawn closed by her with a rattling sound, on its curtain wire. Thus, despite the bedroom being once again separated from the living area, however Gemma could visualize what mom G was doing based on the various sounds emanating from behind that curtain. First, she had drawn the little privacy curtains on each window out in the living room area, now that actual rays of sunshine began to reach the walls of the house from over the hill.

She could hear when mom opened one of the all-wooden windows in the kitchen area by the attendant rattle and prolonged squeak of metal on rusty metal as she first drew the slide lock to its open position, then the double 'blam' sound produced by the two leaves of the window hitting the wall of the house almost simultaneously. A few rays too were now caressing the privacy curtains that were in the now open windows of their bedroom. There was the click and clack of clothes hangers being rearranged as mom took stock of her planned sewing workload for the day and the thunk of the sewing machine cover being shifted. As she moved to the kitchen, there was the shuffle of dishes being uncovered to be made ready for the days use.

What was it going to be for breakfast, Gemma wondered? They had no refrigerator, so it would be bread baked three days ago, hopefully there wouldn't be visible moss growing on it yet. Would mom just make her sugar water? Or would it be a rare cup of hot chocolate? Sometimes she would get a little citrus peel from gospo boiled in water with brown sugar or molasses. Maybe, just maybe, mom might make her lemon grass tea or even soursop leaf tea. She didn't think there was anything exotic lying around in the kitchen, like salt fish cakes. Mom's salt fish cakes were the stuff that one dreamed of, Gemma acknowledged in her mind. Neither had there been any fresh fish like jacks about the house recently. The fishmonger with accompanying shell blowing last happened about a week ago. She shuddered at the thought of fried fish anyway because she had had a terrible time with fish that was 'juking' when eaten the next day. Her mouth had had a prickling sensation, inside her ears had been scratching and her limbs had involuntary twitching too. One of her teachers had said to her, "Please avoid fish for a while Gemma. It sounds like you got ciguatera poisoning child." No meat would be on the menu today, she knew that to be fact! She had seen that there weren't any tins of mackerel, curried goat, spam or corned beef laying around in their kitchen.

As always, being of a poor family, she had to be content to just get something to keep her stomach from hunger. She smiled to herself at the thought that many of her friends at school and therefore their families too, seem to be convinced that her poor family was well to do. Her poor now dead alcoholic father did own his own business and drove a car but that had not ever translated into money coming home! Anyway, he was gone now having left his poor wife with no money, significant debt and even 'outside' kids who she had to try to help financially in addition to her own. As they say, appearances can be deceiving.

Now she closed her eyes and absorbed the sounds and vibes of the neighborhood. Mom G interrupted her by moving the curtains noisily to stick her upper body into the room, reach under the bed and grab the 'utensil'. She heard her mom's careful footsteps and could visualize her zigzag pattern through the room to avoid putting her weight too heavily on certain weak rotting floorboards. She could visualize how carefully mom would be watching where she put her feet; she still had a visual in her head of mom going down her whole thigh scraped and bruised through a collapsed floorboard and urine going everywhere. At the time it happened a couple of years ago, she and her much older sister Mavis, did not know whether to laugh or cry. Of course, they prayed that mom hadn't hurt herself too badly as they rushed to help her. They had shepherded her to the standpipe to help her clean up. It had been a puzzle as to why mom had not said a word. Then, a little belatedly they'd understood why, after she had gotten both her hands and face cleaned. They both then got a thorough tongue lashing even though they felt that they'd had nothing, absolutely nothing, to do with her taking a tumble! The truth is that she either had heard them giggling or knew they were giggling at her misfortune inside their heads. Thank God it was only number One! Then the creaking as the two separate halves of the wooden back door opened, each with a squeak as the two metal hasps were pulled back. There was more creaking as she smoothly descended the three steps, the 'knock knock' and dragging sound as she tapped her sandals on the few stones strategically placed to go up the slight rise to the outhouse. The harsh crashing sound of the latrine door as it was opened and then closed. Finally, the outdoor water pipe came on and Gemma knew that the 'utensil' was getting its all-important ablutions with its special cleaning brush and soap. There was a bottle of Jeye's disinfectant to sprinkle around afterwards. It had such a strong of creosote scent plus whatever else, that even if it did not kill germs, your nose would feel like it did.

Now as she continued to lay on the bed eyes closed, she heard the grinding whine of the big board bus 'Sweet Roses,' Mr. Alban's colorfully decked out steed picking up his loyal customers when they needed to get to their bank and government jobs in the city of Fredericktown about one and a half trundling hours away. Newer minibuses had recently been making inroads into his clientele since they were smaller, more maneuverable, faster, getting folks there up to half an hour earlier. Of course, those new little zephyrs could not carry the kinds of loads that the colorful mostly female market salespeople needed to cart around. About the only thing those big wooden buses didn't seem to take were the bags of charcoal that often involve male salespeople who were themselves as blackened and disheveled as their bags of goods were. Those were often seen tied down in the trunks of jitneys, lorries, pickup trucks or the old wooden buses that had been converted to trucks.

Mr. Branson must be leaning out his back door calling to his fowls, "Come, come get it." Gemma could hear the scrape of a spoon on the plate as he was likely feeding them a few leftover grains of rice from his last night's meal. Unbeknownst to the poor birds, they always got much less than they wanted and were asked to pay a much higher price than anticipated. He did this morning after morning, just so that they'd learn to come when he called. Amusingly, all of the neighborhood chickens were often drawn to this illusory and very scant free food and the poor things would scramble around in the dust competing with each other. Mr. Branson in the meantime was looking at them to select his next meal which he grabbed at will, whether a particular chicken actually belonged to him or his neighbor. So, in essence the fowls were doing an audition to see who would get eaten next, with cocks being most valued. Hens laid eggs and would be deferred until hard times demanded their visit to his pot. So usually, the smart neighbors who worried about their fowls would all stick their heads of their windows, hoping to deter him from swiping their birds. The neighbors all knew that when you passed by his house and smelt a delicious meaty meal cooking, to go count their chickens. To give him some credit though, he was a phenomenally good hunter and had a few well-trained dogs. If you went on a night's hunt with him, you'd be sure to get to enjoy some good manicou (possum) or tattou (armadillo) the next day. So, the man wasn't all bad, even though he was a truly brazen thief and would grab your chicken and wring its neck in front of you with nary an apology!

The neighborhood was definitely stirring. There were four houses fairly close by to mom G's. The closest was the noisiest, Ms. Cici who was nice in her own way, but had trouble understanding degrees of separation. She was convinced that mom G's house was simply an extension of hers and therefore could waltz in at will. It seemed likely that she behaved that way with other neighbors too. Gemma was hoping that they weren't the only family picked out for such special attention! She was extremely gregarious and knew everything, yes, every single significant thing that happened in their little village of Zion and the nearby villages too. To say that she was the village clearing house for gossip would truly not be exaggerating. Well, Gemma could hear her now singing and not softly, inside her house, some kind of spiritual song. The ethos there would be that if I'm not asleep, it is my duty to ensure that all my neighbors are fully awake too. Gemma couldn't help but giggle at the memory of them going to church for a nighttime service while there was still a little glow from the setting sun. Ms. Cici had been caught in a predicament of needing 'to go' urgently and still some distance from the church building and its lavatory and too far from home. So, she had made the hasty decision to squat in the bushes for a quick number One. Lo and behold it happened to be on the edge of Mr. Worley's property. Now no one saw the gentleman sitting still in his low chair dwarfed by the intricately carved concrete railings lining his veranda and his large cherry tree. The veranda was also elevated relative to the road they'd been traversing, making it harder in the semi darkness to spot him. So mid-stream, to hear his booming voice suddenly exclaim loudly, "You can pee, but don't shit" was beyond alarming. One can only imagine what effect that would have had on poor Ms. Cici, mid stream no less. Needless to say, among the few of us with her, this statement has over the years been repeated as a hilarious refrain at every opportunity to each other, especially on the occasion of needing to go.

The other three sets of neighbors were the Renwick family who lived further up the hill in their huge well-appointed home filled with furniture imported from America. Mr. Renwick had visited one of his daughters, step-daughter to be precise in the USA and was smitten with the style of homes and most importantly, the furnishings. When he returned to the island, large shipments followed him back. It had been a sight to see in their little village of Zion. Multiple trucks laden with goodies arriving at one home carrying stuff from the docks in Fredericktown the capital. He had gone about a complete renovation of his already large by Grenadian standards, home. So, there were two master bedrooms for him and his madame and these were elaborate with en-suite everything. Each master bedroom in addition to master bathroom, had both fancy tubs and shower enclosures, plus their own sitting area. Then there was a huge dining room with a super large dining table able to seat twelve. There was a separate family room and living room. He had separate maid quarters, mud room, washer and drying rooms and even a roof top lookout deck plus large wraparound verandas front and back. His house was located on a wide overlooking hillock with lots of surrounding lands with cattle grazing and abundant crops of cocoa, nutmegs, spice trees from which cloves were harvested, cinnamon trees which volunteered their bark to flavor baked goods, coconut, breadfruit and tons more. Most importantly to Gemma, was the wide assortment of fruit trees growing all over. Therefore, he really did have a mini estate with an 'honest to God' grandiose estate house. Of course, his maid doubled as a concubine too, Gemma mused.

Then there was poor Mr. Walden who lived alone in a rickety wooden shop from which he sold consumable goods in bulk with his doorstep right on the public road. It doubled as his place of abode too! So, he did have his own little niche market carved out, as compared to the other neighborhood small shops which sold to all comers and in small quantities. Unfortunately, that meant that the inside of his establishment was even more packed floor to ceiling and in shambles than the outside appearance of the building suggested. Gemma's lips puckered in a rueful smile at the time she had had to go visit him when he was sick, after she heard him moaning inside there as she walked by. So having returned to her own home to let her Mom G know what she had heard, and knowing they hadn't seen him moving around for a few days, she went to his front door and knocked and knocked. Of course, she had shouted out her name. It took an interminable amount of time for him to drag himself to unlock his front door. Once she saw him, she realized that it had been a supreme effort to just do that. He had been grateful for her help. She had puttered around his cramped living space to find, with him suggesting where to look, some foodstuff for him and his thirty cats, no kidding! After he had recovered from whatever had ailed him, he reverted to his usual gruff and unfriendly self of course. Maybe that was better anyway than fake friendliness, she reckoned.

The final really close by neighbor were two sisters and their youngsters, who were more like Gemma's sister and brother's age anyway. They 'ran' a little neighborhood shop. The public road lay a few feet in front of their doorstep. Their house was situated in essence at a junction point leading to two other sets of villages, therefore there was a fair amount of passing people traffic both on foot and by automobile. Their house though modest, was built with concrete blocks and wasn't the old wooden structure like mom G's so they had the patina of some wealth. They were otherwise quiet and somewhat reserved actually. Across the street, perched on a hillside was a different kettle of fish as they say. Most of those homes were small and shanty-like and the people in them were all characters mostly of the strange flavor and not what one would describe as fine and upstanding! They ranged from flashers flaunting their nakedness for all to see under the pretext of running to the outdoor facilities to outright frequent no holds barred fights! She giggled at how much she had to wrap herself thoroughly in her towel to transition from her own outdoor shower to get back into the sanctuary of her house, for fear of the hard-working peeping Toms and Anns!

Awakening from her reverie as she heard mom G banging a pot and then heading out the back door, she knew that the charcoal fire was about to be lit and breakfast preparation to commence. There was a crinkling sound as she walked and it sounded like she was carrying kindling - old newspapers to get things going. Then Cereal's pleading whine followed by the frantic scratching of his claws as he raced around the yard sniffing and squirting urine then the sounds of him coming up the back door stairs. The rattle and squeak of the back door as he was able to fully open it and enter since mom G had only pushed it closed. He was a clever dog, almost human really in his behavior Gemma thought. There he was nuzzling her fingertips, having snuck quietly into the bedroom. She opened her eyes and he was immediately staring deep into her eyes, tail whipping vigorously. Cereal was clearly saying nonverbally, 'get up, getup, let's go, no time to be in bed!' Gemma said, "Hi Cereal, go play, I'm not ready to get up yet." Instantly, his tail wags slowed, and tail drooping he turned slowly, furtively looking back to see whether his poor-me-one look would elicit any sympathy. She motioned for him to come with her fingers and he again nuzzled her fingers and she rewarded him with a few good pats on his head. Now, all was forgiven as he turned smartly nails squeaking on the old rough wooden floor going back into the cramped living dining room and she heard him scampering out the back door. Hard work was part of a dog's life trying to persuade their dumb captive human two-leggers to go on the sniff and hunt. So obviously Cereal was running off to make the rounds of the neighborhood by himself.

The aroma of warmed up fried bakes with a hint of salted codfish filled the air as mom G returned from outside and laid the hot frying pan on the countertop with a crashing sound. Then as breakfast cooled, the sounds of her vigorously stirring liquids in plastic cups confirmed the imminent call to eat. It was now a little after seven am. When the call came, Gemma was ready, her stomach doing a few growls in advance. At the table, breakfast turned out to be unusually good. There was in fact no real codfish to accompany the bakes, just the scent and indeed flavor too, as mom G had used yesterday's grease residue that was suffused with it to refry this morning's goodies. It was a far better breakfast than Gemma could have hoped for and mom G had made her a cup of her barely sweet lemon grass tea to boot, just the way she liked it. Mom G had made herself orange peel tea this time, although definitely sweetened. Funny how mom G kept a pile of whatever citrus fruit peels that were unfortunate enough to enter her house tied up in a loose bundle on a string hanging from the rafters drying, not far from the cured hambone used to flavor soups. There was a need for great culinary ingenuity living in the shadow of the rich.

Mom G reminded Gemma that after school, she'd need to make a foray into 'the cocoa' to bring some food for the old lady called 'Say-say' who was terribly nice and told incredible stories about the past happenings, many of which seemed to be fantasy though. Those 'Nancy stories' as people around here called them, were sometimes scary and sometimes not. What Gemma knew though, was that often afterwards she'd dream of amazing things for many nights thereafter. She needed to be very careful though that as the old lady regaled her with those stories, that too much time wouldn't slip by. That would not be good. She had to cross two small rivers, really more like creeks, though they could be treacherous enough to break a leg in. The whole area was full of very tall dark trees among which someone who was up to mischief, could easily hide. She didn't want mom G to have to raise a village search party complete with masanto bottle torches fueled by kerosene and burning a cloth wick, to have to come find her in the bush. Those like the huge Mamie apple fruit trees had huge thick dark green leaves that conspired to cover up what little sunlight there was. It made five - thirty in the evening seem dark, more like seven o'clock, when you're deep inside 'the cocoa'. Gemma vowed to carry mom's little torchlight with her today. Her planned excuse to get away from the old lady a little quicker despite a part of her loving and part dreading her tales, would be that she had to go by 'pan-cup' to buy a bag of charcoal.

She liked to think of Mr. Pan-cup as the angel of fire. There was always a glow from several slightly raised mounds of earth that he patrolled with a long rake like pole and a bucket of what looked like dirt with which he darted from mound to mound covering up the glowing portholes into his inferno. Once when she had gotten brave enough to say to him, "Sir, why do you rush to cover the holes?" He stood in one spot, looked at her, took his pipe out from between his severely blacked teeth, the few he still seemed to have anyway and said, "Little gurl, too much air get to the wood and it burns up, no get any coals you hear! You think I run to close the holes for fun now?" It was then she realized that to leave the logs only partly burned, it needed to be starved of air while buried under the mound of soil and that it was a very delicate balance to get the fire going on what was after all, fairly green wood in order to produce actual charcoal rather than having it completely burn down to ashes. Previously she hadn't thought about the process in detail and was even a bit annoyed when she'd get there, maybe even with other people ahead of her waiting to purchase as well and the angel of fire would suddenly look up, grab his metal hooked pole and bucket and go flapping away toward his glowing mounds. That explained why each coal pit took almost a whole week to simmer in the ground and why he did the pits close to the creek as lots of water was needed and quickly, to extinguish the fire once the pit was opened. He often needed the help of some of his neighbors to make a line of fast-moving buckets of water to get the job done. From what she'd heard those neighbors and hangers on got their pay in charcoal. Then the charcoal had to be spread out over a wide area to dry out and make sure that there wasn't even a small remaining ember, as that could get the whole lot burning again. She did have to confess to liking to smell the heady aromatic scents that emanated from the mounds though; it was so fragrant in a burnt heavy sort of way! The odor was quite strong too when the pit had just been 'wet down' as Mr. Pan-cup pointed out. He did confide in her once that there were some very sought-after trees most suitable for making charcoal, but he did not elaborate in detail. She giggled to herself at the thought that suddenly came into her mind; she preferred it to the heavy overly sweet yet stinky sweaty perfumes that the usually fat ladies wore at funerals. That was a truly obnoxious scent mix that her mother often subjected her to, by virtue of dragging her along to funerals. Mom very much fancied going to pay her last respects to people she knew in addition to people who were known to other friends of hers. Gemma got dragged along at every possible opportunity to those festivals of hot sweaty moaning, bawling processions. It was though, quite humorous to see at the end when the body was finally lowered into the grave how there was always someone trying to heave themselves in and having to be restrained by the crowd. That was the fun part really, for her at least. There hadn't been any shenanigans like that at her father's funeral. His drinking buddies had broken a couple of bottles over his coffin, purportedly spilling his 'first love' rum with him in the grave, but she just couldn't imagine that those buggers would have wasted their good spirits that way. She was convinced that there had been more water than pure rum in those bottles!

'The cocoa' was a good mile and a half away and accessible via a serpentine trail. Gemma was hoping that maybe she could entice one of her school friends to go with her soon after school ends at 3 pm. She planned to ask Margarette or Eslyn. Margarette lived up the hill across the street from her and was already along the path that she'd have to take to get there. Eslyn would have to go more out of her way since she lived down in Potry not far from the beach a solid half a mile away. However, she traditionally was more inclined to be adventurous and interested in going on such trips. She would be linking up with her two close friends at nine in the morning when school commenced. There was a twinge of sadness at the thought that her two friends along with herself were going to be transitioning to Secondary School in September. Those two were unfortunately going to be going to the same McDuff High School and she was scheduled to attend Mt. Rush. She would miss them. She didn't want to really face the reality of the fact that they would grow apart, develop new friends, but her mom and even Dr. Benny had educated her to prepare for that. She was even more sad for the youngsters who had not passed the common entrance exam. This is what allowed entry into high school. Those kids would have to finish Primary (Elementary) School and hopefully pass their School Leaving Certificate in Standard seven class to have a piece of paper to their name. Thence they may go on to a trade school to acquire skills in the trades, whether that be agriculture, fishing, carpentry, welding, husbandry or in the hospitality industry to work in hotels. Some may just apprentice with various tradespeople. Others will likely just drop out, make babies, take over their parent's lands or fishing boats, truck or private bus driving.

Chapter 3.   School Day

So, when she finally left the house and reached the end of her driveway she heard a familiar voice calling out to her that was instantly recognizable. It was one of her best school friends Randall, on the way to school too, but on the other side of the street. He had his usual wide smile and didn't seem to be mousy in anyway to her. Why people called him 'Mouse', she remained clueless. He did have a slightly squeaky voice, so just maybe that was the reason she thought. "Hey Gemma, what's up?" He asked.
She replied a little petulantly, "My mom wants me out of the house, so I'm going to school! How are things with you and your

family?" By then he had looked left and right, crossed the street and they started walking side by side. It was Friday morning and the evening and weekend lay ahead. He asked, "Do you have plans for this evening after school?"

She answered, "Yes, mom has me going to do her 'help the poor' chores, as if we aren't poor too. I've got to bring foodstuffs and a cooked meal to 'Say-say' up in 'the cocoa' after school, then I have to swing by 'Pan-cup' to get two tins of coals right after."

He was such a sweet young man, "I would like to go with you Gemma if you need help and if my mom agrees. Of course, once I say it's with you, there won't be a problem you know."

Gemma said, "I hope you can come with me Randall because it's a long trip with heavy bags both to go and to come back. I would feel safer with you going too."

Gemma wore her hair in two long dark brown ponytails streaming down her back this morning. Often, she would wrap those 'tails' around both sides of her head from the back to the front and then back almost like a Gemma crown, giving her a rather distinctive look compared to her peers. Yes she was blessed with uncharacteristically long hair compared to most village girls that were her compatriots. It wasn't such a blessing though when it had to be combed. Her scalp soreness had taught her since from her earliest years that beauty came with pain. She was a skinny cute young lady with big eyes, slightly taller than average and quite energetic. She was quite pale skinned since her dad had been a tall skinny beanstalk of a half-white man although her somewhat plump mom was much darker toned. As a younger kid, she remembered desperately trying to fit in with her much darker toned classmates and colleagues by frying herself in the sun as much as possible. She ruefully thought to herself that being teased with 'whitey bakae, skinned back taetae', a strange phrase of unknown origin targeting the lighter skinned persons, used to feel like rejection of the highest degree. Now she did not get called that anymore since she was old enough to defend herself with threat of pugilistic violence and she was one of the bigger girls now in school! She however was proud to be in the top five of her class academically, very friendly and easy to get along with. She thought to herself with the slightest twinge of jealousy that definitely she was not as friendly, vivacious and garrulous as Marybelle, one of her fellow classmates.

She had on her black 'poonkasol', airy cheap cloth shoes and her book bag was strung around her neck by the straps with it slapping gently against her right hip. It was a sturdy little leathery bag and comfortably held all of her books. It could have held a lunch too, but she really lived only several hundred yards from the Zion Primary School even though it couldn't be seen directly from her house. From her house though, they could hear the noise and hubbub of the schoolyard easily enough. Cricket matches broadcast their sixes and bowl-outs, as did soccer match goals with loud roars easily heard at her home. Children screaming out during intermission times and especially at games sounded quite loud in fact. The loudest assault to the ears came whenever the school hall was being rented out for bingos, political rallies or even dances, the harvest and even the few carnival events that passed through. So yes, the school was of multipurpose use in every way. While she had been stepping down the driveway moments before, she was thinking that soon the harvest and the carnival celebrations would be arriving.

Harvest was without doubt the largest festival and fair, held in the village. Since the village of Zion lay at the juncture of multiple other village roads and along the main road that circled all around the island nation too, their harvest drew attendance from all over the nation, including visitors from the capital city of Fredericktown. Hundreds of buses and cars normally had to find parking, mostly along the streets. Vendor stalls were usually packed chock-a-block throughout the recreation grounds, the Catholic Church yard as well as the Zion schoolyard. This was of course a major fundraiser for both the church itself and its church supported primary school which Gemma attended. Many of the vendors were supposedly donating the proceeds made, though lining the streets further away from the church-yard were many who were 'gypsies' hoping to simply capitalize on the crowd to make money for themselves. Everybody showed up, often 'dressed-to-kill' as people would say; to see and be seen was the order of the day. Lots of folks, especially young men and women just showed up to 'lime', which involves standing around gossiping or slowly oozing along with the waves of people traipsing from stall to stall. Maybe they'd get to see old acquaintances and to 'chit-chat' for a bit. Oftentimes they'd gossip about those who had gotten 'tabanca', referring to the depression mixed with shame that visited persons who had gotten dumped in a relationship. Whatever their interest, people thronged the neighborhood with some coming for the inevitable big dance party that always followed later that night.

Although there usually was music during the day, it was the dance music going on until 4am at the harvest that always proved to be the most disturbing to the sleep patterns of the whole village though. Gemma always breathed a sigh of relief when harvest was over with its noise and drunkenness. Unfortunately too, there were the occasional brash drunken young men who came to make a 'bacchanal'- a fight.

 Carnival was even more of a huge celebration, but it largely impacted the capital city and a few of the official towns of some parishes. Zion had to make do with a few passing bands of roaming colorful polka-dot short-knee who were masked masqueraders showering onlookers with white talcum body powder, jab jabs with their oiled bodies all painted black and the odd ole' mas group or individual. Gemma was quite enchanted too by the odd one-man-band raconteur who could, upon finding a receptive audience, particularly ones who would drop money into his satchel, recite oodles amount of history of the islands going back hundreds of years. This usually took the form of a performative and demonstrative dancing narrative with rising and falling cadences to the sound of slapping sticks, dancing, prancing and most importantly spittle flying! It was captivating how rapidly they would recite the history, reminding her of the drone of auctioneers that she'd heard over the radio, only far more animatedly. She looked forward to the odd may-pole dance performance group, wild Indian dancers and even steel-bands playing atop trucks with accompanying elaborately costumed dancers that may sometimes stop to perform in the junction and the schoolyard area to entertain the villagers who would approvingly come streaming in like ants from their nests.

Randall or 'Mouse' was in the same position as Gemma, marking time for four more months in Elementary school until transferring to the big High School. They had both passed their common entrance exam and for that matter had finished their First Communion a year ago together at the community Catholic Church under Father Michael's watchful guidance. So, they often met both at school and in church. In many ways, they had grown up together especially being the children of two ladies who were themselves good friends living less than quarter of a mile away from each other and they were currently same age. She had thought of still asking her other two girlfriends anyway, in case they turned out to be really wanting to get out of their home and chores.

The two of them walked by Mrs. Margery and Mrs. Ormsbury standing on the steps of the still closed tiny village post office. They were whispering conspiratorially into each other's ears. Gemma thought she overheard the words, "I am sure it was him, absolutely sure it was him. That 'Pan-cup' is a dealer man. Of that I have no doubt. Mrs. Julia too is a ligaroo; my neighbor Mrs. Crepe woke up in the midst of being sucked. She had the black mouth marks on her thigh to show everybody. She vows it was Julia's face on the body of a serpent and Julia was smiling, even winked at her when she was finished and leaving. But Mrs. Crepe couldn't move, could not move at all. When she finally could move her limbs and speak from whatever drug these ligaroos administer, she screamed out. That's when her son and granddaughter woke up and came to her aid. Then a mile away, Mrs. Julia's neighbor caught her that same morning at 4 am walking briskly in her yard. He had just come back from changing his two cows from one field to another, a bit earlier than usual, because he had to go sell in the market. When he asked her what she was doing outside so early, she answered that she couldn't sleep and came out to skip rope. He did see her with a rope too he said. But isn't that strange to be out skipping rope at 4 in the morning? Anyway, he did not believe her!" Mrs. Ormsbury was shaking her head affirmatively, vigorously. Gemma and Randall nodded politely and said, "Good morning Mrs. Margery, good morning Mrs. Ormsbury," and without waiting for an acknowledgment, scooted by quickly.

After the two youngsters were safely past the two gossiping matriarchs without a scowl or a tongue lashing as were their wont, they felt it safe to look at each other. Normally these two would insist on the youngsters from 'well brought up families' to stop and exchange a bit more pleasantries unless they were clearly in great haste doing the bidding of their parents. That they were allowed to scoot by with hardly a glance, was testimony to the juiciness of the ladies' gossip. Gemma was thinking that indeed Ms. Julia with her very pale skin, red hair, plump but puckered red lips and her naturally sinuous way of walking while casting her head in a fluid way about her left and right, surely was serpent like. In fact, it was very vivid to her at that moment recalling the way their serpent of this morning had behaved. Could this one have been Mrs. Julia caught in the act? The hair on the back of her neck truly and literally stood on alert. She could feel it. There was a moment of strangulating, paralyzing fear that ran through her whole body from head to toe, as much as the rest of her rational brain screamed 'stupid'!

People don't become serpents and back into people again, she forced herself to repeat in her mind. Then she realized that she had slowed her rapid pace to a crawl. Randall, himself looking worried, asked, "Do you think that's possible Gemma, what they were talking about?" Gemma trying to put on a braver face than she truly felt said, "Of course not!" Then looking Randall in the face, she said, "Honestly I hope not. But I too have seen myself and my mom wake up and have black marks on our arms and thighs that we shouldn't have had and that we didn't have when we went to bed. Lots of people get those and swear that it came from Ligaroo sucking them at night. Last year my mom and I both woke up in the middle of the night feeling quite odd and noticed a strange glow up the hillside by Mrs. Delaney's house through a crack in our wooden window. It was like a blob of strange glowing light that seemed to be unlike any typical light that hovered, bobbed up and down, circled around their little wooden house as if searching for away in. Then it disappeared under their roof and what seemed like minutes later reappeared and shot off down the hill. Mom had noticed it first and gotten me up to see the strange apparition. How many times have I woken up and felt as if I could not move, or speak, while inside I was panicking? So, the answer is that I dunno, there may really be something to it, to these strange happenings. What do you think Randall?"

By this time Randall's eyes were as big as saucers and he shook his head slowly. "I am scared about things like that you know. I too have had dreams that were terribly scary and when I shared it with my friends, they all agreed that though it should be silly to believe in things like that, strange things that are hard to explain, do happen. Maybe there are logical explanations for why these things happen to people, but maybe there really are people out there doing some weird stuff too. I dunno, I just don't know." They continued the now short walk to the schoolyard and when some of their friends called out in greeting, they waved back.

Gemma said, "Do you remember when Mr. Walden my reclusive neighbor was shot in the arm as he too was strangely skipping rope or claimed to be, in the middle of the road at four in the morning. He must have scared that person severely it is assumed. The incompetent police never did find the shooter from what I heard and whoever did it must not have been up to any good himself." Randall laughed nervously, "Why do you think it would have been a man necessarily? I am beginning to think that between midnight and four in the morning is the deadly period. Only bad people or a few coming back from parties are out. Some of them may not be in their human form either!" By then they were enveloped in a gaggle of other kids a few older, some younger. Whatever heaviness had been weighing them down, evaporated.

School was actually fun now. It was almost February, and the dry season was on, which meant the ground was dry and the earth cracked into a giant mosaic of crazily shaped blocks. The ants had lots of places to hide from the children's feet. There still were the odd showers early in the morning but very sporadic. The sky would get dark as if about to rain and then disappointingly clear, for the farming folks. Noon came and most kids raced home to get whatever meager rations could be found. The really 'down and out' kids who were identified by certain teachers, whose hair was reddish with protuberant tummies right on the edge of kwashiorkor, got to go to the special lunch program. They got the vitamin reinforced gruel, goodness knows what it was made from, but the awful scent began pervading the school and its environs since ten-thirty every morning when the cook started boiling it; she heard it being called bulgar. The scent was like a rolling pox through the school from that time until lunch, everyday. Randall thought to himself, "We are poor like everyone else but thank the Lord my mom as a teacher and dad as an agricultural extension worker provide enough so that I don't have to eat that stuff." During their fifteen-minute break at ten-thirty in the morning, he had swung up into the bouyee tree (wild star apple) on the edge of the schoolyard and grabbed a handful of green ones. They seemed clean enough by inspection and he had avoided picking ones that looked like they carried obvious streaks of bird or possibly lizard dung. He did wipe off any semblance of dirt by rubbing the little green fruits on his short pants in an area that didn't look too soiled of course. That kept his appetite whetted. Of course, those being green, at the end of it, his lips were just about glued together from the white sticky sap. It was chewing gum without the sweetish flavor. A good long drink of water from the standpipe and he felt good enough to take on another hour and a quarter of boring Mr. Campbell's history lessons. Still, he mused to himself, that he had much better smelling fare awaiting him at home than the gruel that awaited the poor hapless ones looking forward to their school provided lunch.

A few kids brought their lunch and it was wise to vacate the classroom because the overwhelming stench of a warm non-refrigerated lunch sitting in a sealed lunch-can for four hours often was like a stink bomb. That was particularly so if the lunch had cabbage, broccoli, brussels sprouts or onions contained therein. Children would scatter running in every which direction just like the ants erupting from an ant nest mound that he had just been poked with a stick. Stirring up ant-nests was after all a favorite pastime of his. Randall was already in mourning. He had heard that there weren't all those breaks to look forward to, once he got to the big boys and girls school. High school was not going to be fun he had decided, but he would be going there nevertheless in September just seven months from now. It was a foregone conclusion. He did look forward to wearing the High School uniform, looking smart with his big bag of books and hanging out with all the smart pretty girls as they all ended up there anyway. He would not be denied!

Gemma had moved away from Randall as she linked up with three of her girlfriends, Margarette, Muriel and Eslyn. She gave them each a quick hug and enquired about Muriel's parents. Muriel had missed the previous two days of school that week due to having to help her mom who was sick after some surgery. Muriel seemed glad to have been asked. She said, "Mom is better, but can't lift anything heavy yet. There is a lot that her doctor told her not to do. Dad has to work and so I have to help with everything, from cooking to washing, even carrying water from the standpipe. Dad does as much as he can when he gets home from work though. Even my little sister, the lazy bum, has actually been trying to help a bit since she saw Mum in so much pain. So nice of you to ask Gemma." Gemma said, "Oh I knew you had some situation and had to miss school but I didn't realize your mom had had to have an operation, Muriel. I would surely have come over to help, even if only to help you fill up the buckets of water." Muriel said, "Things are better now at home, but thanks."

Then Gemma herded her little group off to the side and told them about her and Randall's walk from home and the conversation they'd overheard. "So here we are Randall and I minding our business walking to school and we see Madam Ormsbury and Mrs. Margery 'tek and tek' together, water couldn't flow between them, they were that close to each other, talking about Pan-cup being a dealer-man and Mrs. Julia being a Ligaroo." All the girls chirped in together, "I knew it." They said that almost in unison. There was a tension, a nervous tension humming like electricity running through the group. Muriel said, "Mommy had suck marks all over her and the doctor had told her that she had low blood. He didn't believe that it was Ligaroo suck her dry when my mom told him that though. He said no, she was losing blood. He told her that he would cut her and she wouldn't lose any more." Margarette chimed into say, "Yeah we don't have a choice but to go buy coals from Pan-cup but my dad and mom both told me to always go up there with company. So, I watch him like a hawk when I am around him. He seems to treat people with respect, but you never know. I don't want him or anybody else to take my soul." At that, Eslyn said, "Pardon me Margarette, but if you had gone to first Communion your soul would have been safer you know." To which Margarette retorted, "You Catholics, you and your trust in the Pope and Father this and that, we don't do that in our religion girl, we trust directly in God and the Bible, his written word." The playful cuff from Margarette missed its mark widely as Eslyn danced away. Those two have sparred frequently about religion ever since Margarette and her family had converted over to the Seventh Day Adventist faith a couple of years ago. Eslyn a year older than the other three as well as being tomboyish and quite outspoken but in a genuinely fun sort of way, was one of the few who could amiably bring up topics like that and still keep it light and fun. She was certainly a unique bird, as they say. Gemma admired her while thinking, 'man it will be interesting to see where Eslyn would end up later in life!'

Gemma remembered the time that Woodruff, a known terrible prankster tried his terrible joke on her. Now everybody knew of his nasty games and it just so happened that super smart Eslyn had found out on the rumor mill what to expect. Gemma was internally bursting with mirth as the memory had jumped into her consciousness from just watching her antics. So, it had been a much-anticipated spectacle to see what would happen when Mr. Woodruff tried his tricks on Eslyn, with him not knowing that Eslyn was 'in the know'. He'd used different ruses but, on that occasion, best she could remember, while carrying a handful of books he had suddenly stopped on the side of her, and said, "Damn Eslyn, I think I may have forgotten my pencil on the desk. Can you do me a favor and check my left side pant pocket for it?" Eslyn had said quite innocently, "Sure Woodruff!" With that she reached over, slipped her right hand into his left pocket. The next thing to happen and there were lots of eyes to witness this in the school yard was 'Ole Woody' seemed to go ramrod stiff with a very pained look on his face and Eslyn had this intense look of malevolent concentration on her face. Neither of them moved for close to two minutes.

Then Eslyn victoriously said, "Now Woodruff, have you had enough yet?" He winced and in a very diminished voice said, "Yes!" There was a general tittering throughout the crowd of girls that exploded into raucous laughter as finally it burst into everyone's consciousness that Eslyn had smartly turned the tables on the mischievous tyrant. Woodruff was relying on poor little naive girls violently retracting their hands when they touched something soft cold tipped hanging out in his pocket through a deliberately cut hole and then being intensely embarrassed, rushing tearfully to wash their hands from the 'ick' factor. Madame Eslyn instead had grabbed the 'toe tee' as she called it, very tightly and painfully and hung on, much to his chagrin. He knew instantly that he had been had! That was the end of that. We believe that he never did try that ploy on unsuspecting girls again. Everywhere he went for weeks afterward, the much-chastened Woodruff had to deal with smirks, knowing smiles and open ribbing. There were little ditties made up that were sung in his presence. "Who got their petard hung up in a hand?" was one that seemed particularly painful to him but was beautiful to his previous victims. We did not have to insist on Eslyn going to the bathroom to wash her hand either. She did wash them many times but only after he had left the scene with his 'tail between his legs'. One for the record books she had thought.

Gemma looked at her friends and said, "Now you all have me even more scared with this discussion about jumbies and dealer-men, mama maladee, lajabless, soucouyant, ligaroo, plus the devil sitting along with obeah men in between the roots of the silk cotton tree and I have to go this afternoon after school to get two tins of charcoal from Mr. Pan-cup. Who is going to go with me?" Gemma said this already having an idea that Randall may come, but she felt more company would be better than less and there was always a slight chance something could happen to make him back out. Mischievously she also wanted to see if her friends would be too scared to volunteer to go. Shockingly, they all immediately volunteered to ask their parents except for Muriel of course, understandably. So, they agreed to meet at four-fifteen sharp that afternoon at the schoolyard and leave from there together. There was some comfort in numbers. The more the merrier! The first bell rang, that was the warning bell, so they all headed for their common classroom together. They noticed Mr. King standing in the front of the building bell in hand looking at his watch. There was a bunch of younger girls mostly from Standard 3 and Standard 4 playing a quick game of Netball with Teacher Erma brooding over them. She had actually joined their impromptu game briefly. Obviously as the Netball coach, she was prepping her next bunch of girls for competition as many of her team from standard five would soon be gone, transitioning to High School. Then as they entered the main hallway, and were loitering a bit, the second bell went off and the scramble to get into their classroom and take a seat ensued. The partitions had been drawn between the classrooms and in this wide-open area with all standing at attention, the National Anthem was sung and a brief Prayer said before settling down to business.

Eslyn despite the brave front that she wore, thought about the story that Gemma had relayed. She was uncomfortable with those things. Since she could remember, she had had terrible nightmares. Most of them involved her falling; falling off trees, off banks, off the bus and doing so seemingly forever. It sure seemed forever until she woke up herself to loud moaning or worse her own screaming. It was not unusual for her mom or her dad to come into her bedroom area, since it wasn't a full bedroom, more like a hallway in their little home, to wake her up and out of it. Both her mom and dad had shared with her that when they were growing up, they too had suffered from the same thing. Dad would pull her in for a tight hug and hold her there until her heart stopped jumping out of her chest. They both tried to tell her that she would gradually be able to will herself out of those 'falling' terror situations and gratefully she had already noticed that when her dreams started heading in that direction, she could wake herself up and then go back to sleep. Her mom and dad were very close to her. They were extremely good parents, loving, thoughtful, nurturing and in every way supportive. Her dad was the principal of a High School in Granvillevale and her mom a senior worker at a branch of Barclays Bank in the same town. She had one older brother Sebastian and he was on the cusp of turning eighteen. Sebastian was about to finish High School in a few months and embark on Financial Studies at University of the West Indies. Eslyn's family conducted very mature adult conversations and diverse discussions 'no holds barred' and she was very much involved in those. He pointedly told her that little girls often grow up into crazy teens, and that the best inoculation against that was brutal honesty and a keen insight into what makes real people tick.

Therefore, everything that happened to his precious daughter and son, at school, walking home, in church, in their garden was up for unfettered discussion with everyone able to comfortably contribute. Eslyn was therefore, at eleven years of age, far more perceptive and open, yet more sharply discriminative than most of her peers. That opinion of her was shared by all who knew her, her own friends, teachers and neighbors. She knew this to be true too, based on the cringing she would evoke by her sometimes scathingly honest and insightful arguments and observations while conversing with her colleagues. They certainly weren't used to that and said so. Recently she had noticed that many of her close friends were beginning to be more adventurous mentally as evidenced by their level of conversation and she understood that her influence plus their burgeoning self-confidence, having passed their common entrance exams, likely contributed. Discussions within her family always took a scientific tack on this 'jumbie, ligaroo, dealerman issue'. It was as if, even within her own unique family, there was an acknowledgement that on an emotional level it was scary to discuss those issues. Cold scientific analysis was definitely like berthing in a safe harbor.

However, some of the people at school and in her life were so convinced by others and convincing with their own experiences, that she harbored some smidge of doubt yet. That was why when the conversation went this morning to that topic and she began to feel the hair on her neck starting to stand up with her breath feeling hard to pull like when she has her terror dreams, she adroitly changed the conversation. So yes, it was switched to a discussion of the soul and religion which always, always distracts the mind away from other topics! Her tactic had worked perfectly. But having committed to go this evening with Gemma, there was still a little gnawing thread of anxiety in the pit of her stomach. They did have the luxury in their small home of electricity, indoor bathroom, flush toilet, refrigerator, washing machine and even a telephone, so she would call to speak to both mom and dad to get permission to go with Gemma during the lunch break. Eslyn had been taught to confront her fears head-on and she resolved to have an honest conversation with Mr. Pan-cup later on.

Margarette's thoughts, in a break between their history and geography sessions, strayed to their little group's discussion that morning. She thought, "I know we will end up going to different High Schools and grow apart, but I really like Gemma, Eslyn and Muriel and it has been wonderful growing up with them. I am going to enjoy our little jaunt this evening. I just have to make sure that we get back before dark, because I know how scary it becomes to walk alone. I don't want to have to sing loudly down the extremely dark patch on the way to my home where the trees overhang the road and there are no other houses or lights on that section to shine the jumbies away." Even with a flashlight in her hand, she would see a reflection of light glinting off, for example, the hanging dried leaves of a banana tree and in her mind, with the eerie mix of light and shadows, would be convinced that it was some sinister person or even a jumbie there. There were some super dark patches between the roadside berms down between the trees where the torchlight beams could not seem to penetrate and she then felt certain that there was someone or something looking at her from there, regarding her as bait. So yes, she agreed that she got paranoid in the dark sections of her road at night. Occasionally there would be the rare passing vehicle and she would run full tilt as the glow began to get close enough to illuminate that section of road hoping not to break a leg on a pothole or step on a 'crappo' frog dead or alive. Then once the vehicle drew nearer and she figured that the driver could clearly see her she would slow down to let them pass. Once past her she would rev herself up again to running full tilt in the middle of the road behind it until of course, it pulled away. At least that way she would be that much closer to her own home and she reasoned, safety. Anything to get away from the jumbies waiting to break her neck as she heard they got great enjoyment from. She had even heard that they sometimes appeared as two tall pillars of light and as soon as you were tempted to walk between those legs, they would snap shut on you.

Randall, as soon as he realized that Gemma had hooked up with her girlfriends, gravitated to a few boys trying to get in a few games of marbles before school fully commenced. They were off in a corner of the school yard where it was nice and dusty. Fine dust was of course an asset in the game of marbles. Randall watched intently as the boys, mostly from the lower forms did battle. One boy in particular was extremely accurate, pitching from easily four feet away and knocking everyone's marbles off. His pockets were heavy with his booty. He was relishing his victories while his competitors visibly grew more and more distraught. Randall said to himself that it was a good thing that he no longer carried around marbles. In any case the teachers would take them from you if you were seen brandishing them in class. Confiscation seemed to be teachers' favorite threat against anything that was fun for students, he mused wryly. If you had pretty marbles, they were confiscated. If you brought delicious snacks, once they suspected you were sneaking to eat it, no, just simply brandishing it within the building, they yes, confiscated it. So as the first bell rang, and the games came to a rather sudden stop, the boys including 'Mr. Unbeatable' with his loot, gathered up their marbles stealing off to various hiding spots to conceal them until later, for the never-ending rematch games. There would be marble games at breaks, at lunch and most definitely after school. In the meantime, Randall looked over at the rest of the school yard with various groups of students calmly discussing their escapades and their upcoming plans.

Lunch came and went and the evening session from 1 pm to 3pm started. Margarette's parents were glad she was going with friends and wanted two tins of coals. Eslyn's parents just wanted one tin for emergency backup use that they would store under their house. Gemma was going to buy two tins. They each would be bringing their own crocus bag or fine bag to transport their loot home. Black coal dust was going to get on their clothes for sure. So, during a brief interlude between classes, the young ladies discussed coming for the trip in old trousers so their legs wouldn't be scraped too much by sharp edged coal lumps poking out through their bags. Margarette was going to grab a paper bag with a few pieces of 'hard buns' that her mom had baked two days ago to share. Eslyn was bringing a few slices of potato pudding. 'Whoo whoo' they exclaimed, since her mother's potato pudding with its black pepper was notoriously good. Gemma had volunteered some farine with sugar that she hoped to persuade her mom to let her borrow from her tightly sealed jar. She had asked mom to make some ginger beer too; they'd just have to take turns slaking their thirst from the one little cup! The problem was that mom's ginger was not going to help relieve the burning throat sensation from the peppery potato pudding. Mom's ginger beer was usually strong enough to leave one hoping to find a standpipe for water! Muriel looked forlorn at the discussion around her. Eslyn asked Muriel if she would like to have a tin of coals purchased for her and Muriel said, "You would actually buy a tin of coals for me?" She seemed almost in tears at Eslyn's offer. When Eslyn nodded her head in an affirmative gesture, Muriel could only say, "You all are true friends. Girls, thank you. I will have the money ready to pay you when you get back." So all was set, with fun and adventure in the air but for Eslyn, it was more; it was a reckoning too, as she planned to confront the 'lion in it's den'.

The girls on that Friday afternoon departed promptly and excitedly from school. Their classmates knew that they were up to something. For the whole day, there had been a secretive buzz from their tight little clique. When questioned, all they would say is "we got to get together for a trip to the cocoa later on". Gemma hurried home to get the bag laden with goodies, two pounds of flour and two pounds of sugar, half pound salt, some baking soda, three plastic covered bowls one with fried bakes and fried fish cakes made that day 'that could last' and there was some cooked chicken back and neck with dumplings and callaloo for use that evening. There was the admonishment from Mom G, "don't leave my containers you hear. Let her transfer the food to her plates ok."

All was neatly packed in one of mom's striped nylon shopping bags with two neatly folded fine bags also made of nylon at the bottom of the food containers thus nestling them protectively. These were for Say-say. Gemma double checked that she had the snacks and money for the tins of charcoal. Her bag was quite weighty at the end of all that, even heavier than her usual bag of school books. There will be use for Randall, good boy! He'd better show up!

Randall in the meantime had learned of the planned snacks and would not be outdone. So, he carefully planned out what he would bring. He ran over to one of his buddies who had access to a stinking toe tree vine with good sweet pods, a ripe sapodilla for each of them and to top it off he had sea wet that he'd been ripening. Each of the four of them would get at least five sea wets to savor. Those fruits were all pretty hard to come by, and had involved a journey through Kanhook. He grinned to himself at how dark and foreboding that forest in the back of Zion was. People called that foreboding little forest Kanhook. He would never ever go there alone, but he had joined forces with several bigger neighborhood teens who were well equipped with fine bags and cutlasses plus a long cocoa knife to harvest any available loot. He was hoping that his cousin Gemma and their friends would be pleased to get those treats. He shouldered his little bag and having said 'bye' to his parents and two sisters, set off for a cool Friday evening jaunt.

Chapter 4.   Haunting the cocoa

As he walked back from his home to the schoolyard, he realized
that Gemma, Margarette and Eslyn were already there sitting
next to each other on a low wall in the school yard. Their bags
were all sitting on the same wall, a very smart move indeed he
thought. Any foodstuffs whether in a bag or not would be sniffed
out by insects particularly ants. Thus, resting the good edible
stuff directly on the ground would be an invitation to hordes of
invaders who would be in a very angry mood. There was a good
game of netball going in the yard complete with cheering squads
made up of both boys and girls supporting both sides. The
shouting, cheers and whistles punctuated with loud "no" and
shouted "yes, give them, slam it" grew more deafening as
Randall drew nearer. Each team had a mix of upper-class ladies
and younger ones too. Several teachers were present and very
involved with the cheering. The netball coach and her backup,
both female teachers too were fiercely presiding. The piercing
screech of the umpire's whistle emphasized each point scored!
The thump and slap of ball on hands had a strange rhythm, 'tap,
plop, slap, thump' along with the 'scratch, tap-tap-tap of feet
hitting the asphalted tarmac as the players raced back and forth,
braced themselves, cupped hands together then race to the net,
jumping like jack rabbits to slap or slam the ball back over. The
young ladies were constantly on the move, skipping sideways,
calling out to each other, running forward and back, sometimes
getting into partial kneeling positions to brace for a low ball. It
was graceful yet rough ballet with the side preparing for the ball
on the other side also doing their constantly shifting dance. It
was a beautiful thing to behold, really a beautiful dance of
coordination. For a long moment as he got to the edge of the

cheering spectators lining all around the makeshift 'netball court', he was drawn in like everyone else, as if mesmerized.

A few minutes later there was a quiet moment, an interlude which gave everyone a moment to relax from the tension of the game and his eyes went to his friends. He hurried over to them. "Folks we must go, it's getting late," he said. "Look who's talking, you all. We've been here waiting on you and you come now hurrying us up," said Eslyn unsurprisingly. They all got up as one, and started gathering their bags. Gemma pointed to her big and obviously heavy sack and said, "You're the man, you take this big heavy one. You have to hold it a certain way so Mrs. Say-say's food doesn't fall out of the containers. Come, come, give me your small bag; I'll carry that, Randall." Without another word after being appropriately chastened, Gemma reached out took his little bag and they started to walk off. One boy against three assertive young ladies stood no chance he reasoned, as he grabbed the two wide straps of Gemma's large red and silver grocery shopping bag and lifted it off the uneven stone wall and swung it carefully over his shoulder taking care to keep the bottom of it level with the ground. He felt and heard the clatter and movements of a few containers and bowls inside it. Gemma turned round to inspect it part on his shoulder and part on his back. He realized that it wasn't so much as heavy as it was just very awkward to carry.

Walking through the milling crowd, they were soon in the clear, walking two abreast with Margarette and Eslyn in front, and Gemma alongside Randall. Through the paved portion of the school yard thence onto an area of short dry looking much trampled pasture grass and then the public roadway designed for two vehicles only to pass in either direction. Then, they were obliged to go single file and even were literally confined to the grassy banks. That was the only way to stay alive when the traffic was flowing, which it was with people in cars, bikes and buses now returning from work. The roads could, in most sections accommodate one vehicle comfortably but two passing each other meant each slowing down considerably and carefully negotiating road space. That often included one vehicle or both putting their tires in the 'bush' off the asphalt. In fact, there were some sections of roads where there were so many potholes that vehicles essentially abandoned the center of the road and created new running paths on either edge. They walked quietly for the next ten minutes paying attention to the traffic until they crossed the street carefully to take a poorly paved road on their right that led uphill.

Traffic here was virtually nonexistent of the vehicular type. Once in a while, a truck or pickup would slowly and carefully venture up that path. It wouldn't be rare to see a farmer riding his donkey or mule up or down that trail. As they ascended into the hilly territory the noise from the main road receded in the distance. There were initially a few modest homes with paved driveways but this gave way to sparse homes and 'gaps' in the foliage through which sometimes it was possible to discern the odd wooden shack. There was life though tied along and sometimes across the road in the form of goats, sheep and cattle. In one case, they had to divert from the main road onto the banks to get away from an aggressive bull that seemed to be having fun. The moment they came around the bend, he stopped chomping on the grass looked up and seemed by his attitude to say 'you're not passing here through my territory Brethren.' He snorted, lowered his head threateningly, snorted and 'showed the whites of his eyes'. They all stopped in unison. First things first, look to see how well secured was his ropes. In this case, he was tied to a really stout tree, and he was restrained with a chain. His owner had done a good job with that part, but a terrible job having him to where he could reach almost across the track.

They decided to get into single file, and lining up one behind the other, they filed into the brush on the side opposite to the bull. They called that 'breaking bush' to get away. All the while, the bull continued its antics of bowing its head up and down and blowing dust up with loud snorts. Thank God, they thought that he didn't make a big rush at them. They would have been mortified that he would burst his chain and crush them. Those two large curved horns would certainly have made short work of them. This was like a walking nightmare. They didn't want to have to think about the return trip and having to once again be getting by this dangerous animal. Randall surmised as they walked by, that maybe it was just purely bad tempered or it had been previously provoked by naughty youngsters to get it to that point. To make matters even more interesting were the many dogs that seem to lay quietly in their master's yards only to rush out at them with loud barking as they drew abreast. Eslyn and Randall both had secured sizable sticks, truly they honestly were long poles that they'd happened upon while they walked. They certainly made a difference in keeping some of those persistent 'buggers' at bay so they didn't advance too close to their legs.

They had gone at top speed uphill and upon reaching a high point known as Voltaire pasture which was sloping yet still had a flat spot in the middle where a cricket pitch was located, they'd stopped. The sunshine was bright there but clearly the sun was lowering in the sky. They knew what that meant. They'd have to hurry, since they now were truly about to descend into the valley between the higher ridges and it therefore would get dark down there under the forest canopy. From there, situated on one of the many ridges that ran downhill from the mountains toward the flatter lands by the sea, they stood to look around. Below them in the distance a mile and a half away they could see where Zion and the surrounding villages to it were located. They stared at the wide expanse of ocean called the Caribbean Sea. There were whitecaps close to land where the wind driven waters broke over submerged reefs.

In the flatlands around the beaches were the settlements with crops of fruit trees, what little small plots of sugarcane still existed for rum production and a few isolated dry forests. Their eyes looked at the very visible stands of coconut trees that have been also growing smaller with the passing years. As their eyes pulled up the rising ridges closer to them, it all looked like a forest of trees. They knew well though that as those 'forests' ascending the slopes toward them and beyond toward the mountain tops were comprised of nutmegs, breadfruit, cinnamon spice along with accompanying wind break trees like mahogany, campeche, silk cotton, hog plum, sweet wood, sapote, seawet, mahoe interspersed with shorter crop trees like cocoa and avocado. In the wild uncultivated patches of previously disturbed lands, they could make out bois canot trees with their large leaves with bright silvery undersides. Thankfully few bright silvery undersides could be seen so the weather would be ok for now. Were it to have been windy, there would be lots of white upturned leaves showing on those trees and that would have been a harbinger of bad weather, at least during the wet hurricane season. They hurriedly opened their snacks and filled their stomachs with the goodies. Randall found a suitable large flattish stone and a smaller one with which to break open the stinking toes he'd brought. They had to take their time with that one snack. The edible portion was dry, powdery and one had to be careful to make sure there was enough saliva to fully moisturize it. Attempting to swallow it while it was still dry and powdery could result in choking or worse coughing with the dust exiting through one's nose. Needless to say, they were expert enough to avoid that indignity. In ten minutes, they were loaded up and heading off the main track into the flattish valley between the ridges.

Randall remarked, "Did you all know that there was a sugar mill close by that old broken-down house near the pasture? Can you imagine what it would have been like to stand on this ridge and look out at nothing but sugarcane fields maybe with a few wind-break trees hundreds of years ago when sugar was king in the Caribbean? Mr. Morgan our history teacher just last year went over how the vegetation on this island would have changed quite a bit from the years of slavery to now. Nutmegs were not big until the last fifty to seventy years as crop diversification became necessary for survival." They all nodded. Eslyn said, "Yes, it's amazing to think that there were probably six or more small sugar mills between here and the coast where we came from. Then the cane juice was boiled down on site to make molasses using the bagasse from the mills for fuel; this molasses would be used locally or be better refined to make sugar granules or rum prior to export to England. African slaves would have been everywhere eating breadfruit and whatever ground provisions they could grow in between their work with protein from fowls, goats, sheep and imported dried fish from the same old England. There were so-called 'great houses' up and down the land, where the privileged lived. Most were gone now, wrecked as the estates got more and more broken up and unprofitable."

They all nodded as they loaded up and started down the narrow path that led toward their final destination in the dark 'cocoa'. They were in dimmed dappled light as soon as they left that partly bald hill, now surrounded by thick dark cocoa trees and larger nutmeg and clove trees plus even larger fruit trees interspersed with mahogany and campeche that acted like wind breaks. There was dappled light filtering through and they stepped over a weakly babbling brook with barely a hop. Uphill for a short while, then downhill again after another four hundred feet across a bigger creek necessitating a slippery downhill set of hopping movements from boulder to large boulder over clear chuckling water with little brown fishes darting to and fro. Gemma had time to make out a few colorful black with red speckled crayfishes amidst the more usual brownish ones. She also saw a few 'suck stones' browsing the submerged rocks for algae and whatever else they fed on. They were then scampering up the next bank and not more than one hundred feet away was Mrs. Say-say's ramshackle wooden unpainted shack. Of course, there would be no electricity nor piped water up here in the bush. So, it was no surprise to see a roughhewn wooden shelf outside holding several buckets presumably full of water. She reminded herself to offer to get clean water in for her.

"Hello there, Mrs. Say-say." Gemma called out loudly. "It's me with some friends." Gemma could detect the slightly sweet yet pungent scent of a latrine left open, somewhere close. The door creaked open and first her old wizened face appeared, peering out with that quintessential smile between toothless lips and then her right hand with her pipe. When she spoke, a slight puff of smoke, obviously pipe smoke floated out from between her lips. Her whole body emerged as she recognized Gemma through her rheumy eyes and spryer than any of them expected, she hopped down the three steps to the ground wearing a very old bodice multi colored with long dirty sleeves frilled at the shoulders and a long multilayered formal looking previously white skirt that ballooned from her waist. Our eyes must have widened in amazement, because she volunteered, "Oh you all seem to think ah de born old! When I was young, much younger, I along with many of my friends male and female, used to get together to have dances, the old lance seirs french style dancing. So, we had to have these long sleeves and low to the ground fluffed dresses. None of my former partners are alive. I am in my early nineties still going strong as the Lord has willed it and so I choose to wear what I want, when I want. I'm not going go with it you know."

With that she cackled a little laugh and took a puff on her pipe. There was a large wicker style rocking chair next to her step and she had settled into it, pipe still in her right hand as she rocked back and forth eyes going from face to face carefully. It was as if she was trying to suck in the very essence of each of her visitors. Gemma thought, "She has to make the most of her visitors since they were likely few and far between." Say-say as if she'd read Gemma's thoughts said, "It's really nice of you all to pay an old lady a visit you know. You all are going to be blessed for doing that. I remember being you age, my parents, poor things, had eleven of us and the oldest took care of the youngest. I was the next to the youngest and we all worked the land, hard. By the time I was ten, there was no more school for me and at thirteen Mr. Nichols son who was twenty-five came to ask my parents for my hand in marriage. Of course, what were my parents to do? It was one less mouth to feed. They didn't last long after that either. They died in their forties. At fourteen I had the first of six children. Four of them plus my husband too, are gone now. Two of them still look back and help with what they can. I have thirty-two grands and I don't know how many great grands. Some visit, some I have never met. So, it is good to meet you all."

She then directed a question at Eslyn the face most unfamiliar to her, "Who is you people little girl?" Eslyn piped up, "I am the daughter of Jonas and Cynthia Cummins. My Dad's parents are Emerlin and Isaiah Cummins." At which point Say-say startlingly launched herself upright from her chair to a standing position reaching out her left hand to steady herself against the wall of her house." She exclaimed, "You don't say, Isaiah Cummins, is that the same Isaiah who went to Aruba. He was a lovely boy. I danced with him once or twice and he was a lovely dancer too. I often wondered whether I'd ever see him again. Is he still with us dear child?" Eslyn said, "Yes Ma'am he does not go out much now, but he is very much with us still." Say-say who had opened her eyes to peer more intently at Eslyn's face said, "You favor him a bit in the nose and general shape of your face and you walk confidently too, as he did. Tell your grandpa that I send my regards and you grandma too. Tell him I enjoyed dancing with him." She let out a surprising little giggle, then set her face in a stern solemn expression. She said, "So there is still one of us dancers left eh besides me, but he was younger than Mr. Nichols and myself." She sat back ruefully staring into the distance at memories that she would never be able to share with them. Gemma thought, "Isn't it odd how those old ladies often referred to their husbands formally as Mister!" To herself she said, "I suppose speaking to children, it was the thing to do so that they'd be respectful when they'd meet up with their spouse." Mrs. Say-say continued to probe Margarette and Randall's family tree for the next fifteen minutes.

Gemma in the meantime made herself busy, after having asked Say-say to be excused when there was a polite break in the conversation. Say-say had waved her hand imperiously when she had been asked where to put things. Say-say, "You put it in the usual places child, you go inside and make space." So up the steps Gemma had marched with the big bag that Randall had dutifully carried, thank goodness. There were several already cleaned utensils with one large metal pot and two lidded plastic tubs. She thoughtfully arranged the cooked and baked stuff in one container and the raw materials in another. Then she came back outside and checked her water buckets. Two were empty and grabbing those she raced over to the little river creek next door and carefully choosing her filling spot scooped up one bucket at a time. She had been careful to make sure that there was no hidden man or woman who could rush in and ambush her. She heard of girls getting raped in the river since she was a child and was very wary.

While the others were keeping Say-say busy talking, Gemma took her broom that leaned against the side of her house and gave her yard a quick vigorous sweep. When she was done Say-say stood up and said, "Gemma, it's getting late, so before you could ask me, I'm telling you to head back now. There are some bread nuts here that I did promise your mom. Thank your mom for me and thank you for bringing your dear friends. I do enjoy you all's company but it gets dark here in the cocoa right quick and early. I know you need to go pass by Pan-cup for your charcoal, so git going now. Your mom would be upset if I don't send you home early enough and quite rightfully so. See you all soon again when you come visit the old lady." We watched as she climbed her stairs and as she started to pull the door closed, we started walking towards the creek. It was nice to feel her bag now virtually empty but for the fine bags to carry the coals and the already cooked bread nuts that she'd had to fill up one of mom's containers with at the end, after Say-say insisted that she bring it home to mom G. "Make sure you bring your friends back later for plums, french cashews, pomme rose and lots of julie mangoes," she said to our rapidly disappearing backs.

Gemma knew where Pan-cup's house was from here, so she told the crew that they were going to 'break bush' to get there faster. 'Break bush' they did and they came up behind his house, right past his pit latrine moving toward the front of his house. They had passed by large stands of fast-growing mesquite as well as glorisita trees that was one of pan-cup's secret to making good charcoal he had told her, when Gemma had asked many months ago. He had only one coal pit actively burning close to the ravine. They had already crossed the bigger creek upon leaving Say-say's place. They really could have followed their noses toward the smoldering distinct scent of his charcoal pit. They did get a few sharp gashes from razor grass for their trouble and admired his stools of crayfish colored sugarcane. He was stooped pushing wood in his fireplace under a superbly blackened thick iron flat pot with some sulphur-colored thick liquid boiling noisily within it. "There must be some curry in there," Gemma thought. Without turning around, he said, "You children come from by Say-say, I have been listening to you all breaking bush for the last two minutes. A ha some nettle back dey, you all eh get tangled up in it ah hope!" Gemma answered, "A few prickles and the razor grass got friendly, but if there was nettle, we didn't see it." He said, "You're a good person, so I hope you missed it. Anyway, you know how to go through bush girl, so if you didn't see it, is good. Who you bring wid you dis time?"

As he got up slowly and turned around, Gemma said, "These are my school friends Eslyn, Margarette and Randall. They heard I was coming and wanted to get coals too." Pan-cup lowered his voice conspiratorially, "Yes, it is wise to bring friends wid you all the way up here in de bush 'cause you doh want lajabless to blow in you face'. Da would make it easier for he to visit you in de night you know. You know he could take de form of a ball of light or come as an animal like a snake too." As he said that his eyes grew larger and darted furtively into the surrounding dark recesses of the cocoa. They stood in his yard which was framed by a decent circle of light yes, but this was hemmed in by a rapidly darkening forest of trees and cultivation.

That was Eslyn's cue as she said, "Mr. Pan-cup good evening I am Eslyn. My Mom and Dad would like to buy one tin, Margarette needs two, Gemma needs two tins, we need one tin for a friend whose mother is sick so she couldn't come and Randall needs two tins please." Mr. Pan-cup stood peering head slightly tilted at her and said, "Girl who you people be?"
She said, "Jonas and Cynthia Cummins." He said, "You mother work in de Bank Barclays?" She said,
"Yes she does work in Granvillevale." He said, "Ah know ha, ah know ha well you know. We does get along good good. Ah ha all me clove and spice money and me nutmeg money in deh and when ah bring me bank book, she does make sure ah get all me interest. You is good people then."

He set about scurrying toward a lean-to made up of large logs protected at the sides and top with plastic sheeting with a large flap to cover the front part. That was where he kept his charcoal after it was fully cured and cooled with no danger of accidentally reigniting. Still, it was a good sixty feet from his wooden house and almost on the banks of the creek. He had to make sure his house didn't burn down by his own charcoal, yet keep it close to his water source. Yet he did not want it too close though, for his stash to be washed away by a freak flooding event from the creek. All these little creeks and rivers could turn into raging torrents of muddy water carrying logs and large boulders since they came from the nearby mountains. It was foolish to underestimate those creeks. Of course now, in the middle of dry season, that was less likely. However, there are rare occasions that rains may fall overnight in the mountains and with no warning the next morning the folks in the lowlands like in the village of Zion could get a nasty surprise. Many peoples' clothes left on stones in a calm river waiting to be washed next day ended up in the sea that way. There was even a story of one woman in the middle of the day, so engrossed with her washing that she ignored the loud banging and crashing sounds of a wall of water coming down the river and she barely escaped with her life only, no clothes. In fact, she was washing in her panty and bra and that's how she had to walk home. The cry of 'river coming down' was one to be taken very seriously indeed. Two other noteworthy cries were to be heard in the village- the blowing of lambie shells to indicate the fishmonger was close by and the same tooting just more frantic, when one eyed Fred was about to blast large boulders with explosives. He was one of few throughout the island legally allowed to handle that explosive stuff. You did want to be far away from that kind of blasting. It was cool though to go by and see the results; huge boulders would be split neatly in two or in several pieces just exactly as he told the village it would be. Rarely did his blasting not result as planned, and then usually due to some previously unknown defect in the internal stone structure!

All tins of charcoal went to bed in their respective bags and Pan-cup wiped his hands on a blackened rag hanging nearby. Pan-cup made sure to pack into his measuring tin with large blocks of charcoal mixed with medium lumps and some smaller ones. Everyone got a nice mix of different sizes. Gemma who had been cooking with her mom G since a small child, could see that the quality was excellent. His hands came away as blacked as before from the wiping! Randall, standing somewhat behind the young ladies, caught himself thinking ruefully, 'why even bother wiping your hands man?' He kept his face straight looking at the money as it passed hands. 'Dammit' he thought realizing that he had not bring exact change. All the others handed their bills over and bent down to toe knots in their fine bags. He took his three paper dollars change and as neatly as he could, slowly folded it and stuffed it into his pocket while grimacing on the inside. Those bills were definitely black with charcoal dust and he would rather not have had to handle it. He'd be washing his hands thoroughly whenever he could. Anyway, they were all going to have black dusty hands, just from having to handle the bags of charcoal surely. There was no way to prevent some dust from seeping through the bags, no matter what one did. He resigned himself to his fate, that of black dusty hands and pant legs too in addition to filthy dollar bills.

Oh dear, Eslyn was not finished with Pan-cup. After all the financial transactions were done, she piped up, "Mr. Pan-cup do you mind telling me your correct name and why do they call you that?"
He slowly turned and looked at her as if debating whether to send the little 'scalawag' off with a stern warning. Then he said when he saw her looking earnestly with no smile, "My real name is John Nesbit and you said you are Eslyn Cummins yes!" She nodded yes and looking him in the eye, she said, "Two of us

overheard two ladies down in Zion talking about you as a dealer-man Mr. Nesbit, is there any truth to that Sir?" He looked puzzled and then laughed out loudly. It started out as a gentle laugh but became a deep belly laugh and ended up with tears streaming down his face that he wiped away with his charcoal filled hands leaving even more wet black streaking all over. He walked over to the steps leading up into his ramshackle wooden house that surprisingly had glass windows and blinds behind them they now noticed. By then he was in a spasm of coughing. The youngsters left their bags of stuff and walked over with him in case the poor man needed help they thought.

Now seated and calm, he looked up at Eslyn. "Young lady, you are one brave little thing! Let's put it this way. I ain't ever dealed anybody that I know of. Unless is something that I do while I'm asleep and can't control. No, I ain't no dealer-man. You see me here, up in de woods working day and nite to make a living. Ah doin' wah most people doh wanna do. Some ah dem people say ting about other people just because they keep quiet and to deh self and doh bother no one and still seem to be doing ok. Maybe is jealousy or deh too idle. And ah doing well good. Ah doh owe nobody, ah treat people fair and ah ha more money in the bank than most people have around here. Now ah ain't telling you dat there ain't people out deh that doh try ting, because there is people who try. I heard first hand of people who try to put themselves in a trance and force themselves out of deh body to travel to other places and do funny ting. Ah sure know of people who ha knowledge of poisons from plants da could make other people bazoody and dotish an make dem see ting da ain't there. Then dey could make their victim do all kind ah ting that they would never do otherwise. So yes, strange ting like dat does happen. Ah de go all me life to shango dance and shango ceremony at Mrs. Georgi and ah see ting wid me own eyes dah kinda hard to believe a man could do. Ah see man walk on hot coals, cry like all kind ah animal, no joke. So is dere strange stuff dat happens, yes most definitely yes. Is de mind powerful? Yes. Do I deal, yes but only in cloves, nutmeg, cinnamon, yams, sweet potatoes and charcoal young lady. Don't let 'Nancy stories' that we de older ones tell you the younger ones to make sure you come home earlier to your safe little homes, make you think it's real. The real evil lies with real live people who can and really do some bad stuff to each other. If you all come back to buy coals and remind me, I'll tell you the story about how some people began to call me 'pan-cup'. Now git on down de road. Is getting late and ah do wanna have to answer to Mrs. Cummins as to why you get home so late ok." He stood up dismissively and we said in unison, "Thank you Mr. Nesbit, good night Sir." He stomped off toward his charcoal storage lean-to, likely to close it off for the night. Gemma thought to herself, 'this is perhaps the longest conversation on his end likely that he'd held for ages'. Certainly, it's the most she'd heard him ever speak in her presence and she had to admit that he was really articulate 'when all was said and done.'

The bunch wasted no time crossing back over the little shallow mostly leaf covered ravine and almost ran up the hill to get back up to that little pasture bald spot where there was still a fair amount of light from the sun which itself was racing to its hot date down below the horizon with the sea. From there with a higher ridge between them and the remnant of the sun, all they could see was its light. Randall had taken the bag of coals due to be given to Muriel and Gemma had her two tins in one hand plus her mom's bag containing empty containers though one of them was now filled with the bread nuts. Margarette had her own bags. She reasoned that they were going downhill all the way and fast. If a few bread nuts jumped out of the container, they were hard boiled still in their shells and thus unlikely to be damaged. She did need to be careful not to bang up the charcoal too much or she'll get home and only have charcoal dust! So, with the bread nuts bag slung over her shoulder and the fine bag with charcoal by her side, it was time to go, go, go. And go they did, it was only when they were within sight of the school yard that they realized that the owner must have come for his 'bull-cow' because it wasn't there to threaten them on the run back. Margarette had already peeled off from them to tackle her trail home. Now it was dusk, but they were back in familiar territory and Eslyn had the longest trek but on roads that she was familiar with and she did have a flashlight. Randall had also given her his stick to fend off any pesky dogs or people too. 'All man to their hole' as they say.

Randall dropped her off and she wished him a safe trip home. Standing for a moment in the edge of her driveway, she turned to watch him disappearing rapidly toward his home taking the left turn at the junction. She could only barely see him as the dusk was getting heavier and the one little street light didn't penetrate that far. She turned her back to the street and saw her mom standing on the steps by the front door looking at her. She knew her mom would be getting anxious by now, which is one reason that had motivated her to ramp up the pace. She walked down the shallow incline then up the partly paved driveway that was shared between them and the famous Mr. Renwick. Mom had stepped further into the yard to meet her saying, "That's a lot of load for you my poor thing and she grabbed the fine bag of charcoal out of her hand, swung around to place it under their house behind the bedding for Cereal. Cereal was in its wagging marathon, and when mom bent down, it tried to lick her mouth of course. "Nasty, that's the same mouth that he was grooming his privates with minutes ago Mom, did he get you?" Mom indignantly answered, "Of course not Gemma!" Mom slipped off his chain from the neck collar and he bolted over to Gemma. Mom G said laughing, "Now you can let him lick your mouth now, just don't expect to eat or drink from my kitchen ever again though." Cereal made his usual attempt to jump up and put his paws on Gemma's shoulder and she gave him 'that look", which he knew well to mean 'do it and die' and he perceptively knew to back down. Instead, he ran around and around her, grass flying where his claws dug in at high-speed, tail up in the air. Gemma reached her right hand out and he came to an abrupt stop with his head under her hand. Gemma gave him a rough tussle at first, then a gentler caressing pat on his head, working her way to scrape gently back and forth over his eyebrows then up and down his snout finally under his chin with a little bit of nail scratching in. Cereal's eyes closed blissfully, head slightly lowered and he was 'still as a mouse'. This was pure pleasure and enjoyment to him. Mom who had been watching him get his petting, walked the few steps over and grabbed the other bag from Gemma saying, "You can't be playing with your dog and handling my grocery bag either young lady. Go wash up and I'll have your dinner on the table ready for you. You can tell me how your trip went while you're eating my dear." Gemma said dutifully, "Yes Mom."

Gemma went inside, got her bath towel and soap, changed from her shoes into a slipper and scooted out the back door to the outdoor shower. Then she scooted back up the hill behind the house to use the facilities. Back in the shower, she let the water run briefly sampling it with her fingers hoping to get a bit of heated water from where the pipe was exposed to the sun. It wasn't a guarantee as sometimes if there had been heavy and recent use by mom or the neighbors who shared that water line, it would then only be 'stone cold mountain water' flowing. She'd lucked out, so she promptly shut off the tap after getting her rag moistened, got naked but for her panties, and soaped down. Then setting the rag aside, she turned the pipe on praying for a reasonable flow of warm water sufficient to completely wash off. Lady Luck smiled and it turned cold just as she got to washing her feet. Then she washed off the soapy rag and turned to see her 'macko' dog Cereal staring at her. She gave him the perfunctory 'mash dog' command, but the rascal, who seemed for whatever reason to be totally taken with observing naked people especially her bathing, only momentarily ducked his head as usual. Almost immediately he was back staring. She mused that he was quite likely a reincarnated 'Peeping Tom' man somehow. Nothing she could do would ever seem to dissuade him. Then again, the shower did not have a closable door on the side facing their home. There were three galvanized barriers to minimize prying eyes from the road and other neighbors, that's all.

He was unique not only in that sphere, but he was also the cleanest dog she knew. He rather disdainfully would step from stone to stone and then up the steps, nudge the barely lockable front door open with his muzzle and walk through the house to get out the back door when it was raining and muddy. At the back door, if he tried and couldn't get it open on his own, he would stand there and stare at whoever human was sitting there until someone got up and opened it for him. He mentally willed folks to notice his needs and do his bidding, all of that so he could walk from the front yard to the backyard without getting dirty in wet mud! At night, he was chained to the house post under the house to prevent straying and guarantee some guarding of his humans above. This did not happen without protestations and his even very humanlike sulking though. Furthermore, she could speak to him about most things and he would cock his head to listen, then do what was commanded. There was hardly anything more he enjoyed than being wiped down with a towel. With the command to him of "go bathe Cereal", he would allow damp application of soap, then he would walk down the two hundred feet to the river that passed nearby, have a swim and shake himself, then return for his reward - the wipe down. He definitely did not fancy the water falling on him from a tap. At 3pm at the end of school, despite having to run the gauntlet of other dogs some of which were unfriendly and aggressive along the way, he would be there at the school yard waiting to escort her home even if she had to stay in a bit later. Being loyal, steadfast and fastidiously clean endeared him to her. Gemma had no doubt that Cereal was a very special dog. 'A special dog for a special girl,' she thought grinning to herself.

A hop, skip and jump, several to be exact got her through the stepping stone gauntlet and up the rickety stairs she went with her bath towel wrapped around as much of her as she could get it to. Of course, Cereal followed right on her heels. The familiar creak and slam of the front door followed with the rattle of the few barely contained slats of glass. Cereal made himself small in a corner curled up, but not too far from her feet. She sat at the little table and mom brought her a glass of juice. They both sat across from each other on a tiny table in a corner of the living dining room. Mom said 'grace before meals' and they ate slowly and talked. Now Gemma generally ate whatever was put before her, with today being no exception. There was rice and peas mixed in with ample vegetables and a smidge of meat, tasting like a piece of chicken back and neck. It was delicious as all of mom G's meals were well known to be, by the whole neighborhood. Mom G was unbelievably good at conjuring up the most delicious oildown, curry meat whether chicken, goat or beef, peasoup, callaloo soup, fried fish dishes, fishcake and saltfish souse. In fact, it was surprising when there wasn't a hungry passerby looping in for some lunch or dinner. They were often mere acquaintances who smelt the food from the road and would call out, "Mom G what are you cooking, it smells so good, do you have enough for me?" At which point it was pointless for Mom G to say anything but, "Come on, we'll find some for you?" That usually meant less for everyone at home of course.

Dinner went on and Gemma related how her school day had gone, what classes they'd done, since there hadn't been time to chat when she'd come home to pick up the stuff to go to 'Say-say'. So, Gemma was able to elaborate on the netball game going on in the school yard, that they'd had to pull themselves away from. There was a discussion about Randall and his much enjoyed treat of stinking toe. Mom G told her how when she was young and living in Mohair, a village not very far away where she grew up, how she and a few friends would visit a group of tree vines when they were in season. Mom G did not get to pass the common entrance exam and instead had had to content herself with going on through Standard Six and Seven before earning her 'School Leaving Certificate.' There had therefore been no High School in her life. Nowadays, everybody sought 'tooth and nail' to get their kids into Secondary or High school with possible College beyond that. Better jobs, like teaching and much sought-after bank sector and more lucrative government jobs could not be had without such credentials. A few even back in her time coming from families with money and status plus a decent brain, had made it to University in the UK, Canada, USA or the University of the West Indies. Without money, even the bright ones had little hope of going that far. She instead had learned a trade, sewing, gotten married and had three kids. Her oldest son had gotten a job, married a local girl, moved on to Brooklyn and was 'making up papers' to get mom G up to the USA, hopefully soon. Her daughter who was working already still lived at home. They were both around ten years older than Gemma who was mom G's little late mistake with her always drunken husband, the watch repairer. Of course, the alcohol had eventually taken his life, having escaped multiple attempts at drowning in muddy waters from falling into drains along the side of the road. Gemma had had to be the spindly little helper at times to her poor daddy when he was flailing down in the drain and she heard him calling for help. He was often seen staggering just like his buddies and drinking partners all across the street, occasionally holding up traffic. Most embarrassing those episodes were to a young girl, not to mention the wife mom G.

About the only thing more embarrassing to Gemma, was going to the local shops by herself. There was no escaping that fate though. Often there were young men sitting on the walls, legs dangling and very idle. It wasn't rare for them to be hangers on awaiting one of their employed friends to come along, to wangle a few dollars or even a drink from them. Or sometimes it would be they themselves had come from their job and were just killing time gossiping or worse waiting to harass young ladies. This was the time when TV was not yet common place of course and even those who had electricity and a set had no usable reception anyway. In fact, Gemma saw taped movies up at Mr. and Mrs. Renwick's place or when someone did a reel-to-reel show at the school for a small fee. So yes, Gemma hated to pass by such gathered groups of idle 'liming' men. She, even though only a child at ten 'straight and skinny as an arrow' with no secondary sexual characteristics at all, would have to hear comments such as, "Go girl, you're coming to come. Looking good, give it a few more years, your pokey bone is nice and high, I'm going to have to teach you this and that etc." The taunting, often very sexualized, was tremendous and horrific. She had learned to fly past at full speed whether loaded with grocery bags or not. When there were groups of kids, the taunting was usually less of course. This afternoon had been blissfully pleasant, maybe those harassers had all been inside the rum shops filling up when she had passed. Also, she was with Randall, that often tempered things down.

Gemma brought her momentarily straying mind back to the table. She proceeded to tell mom G about their journey up the hill done at full racing speed and how they'd shared the load among themselves. The episode with the 'bull-cow' too brought cackling laughter from mom G and the nervous variety from Gemma. Mom G confided that she has over the years had to navigate such scary events too, whether it be cows blocking the roadway, goats attempting to slam their heads and horns into her rear, or seemingly rabid mongooses which lived in a den just up the hill from their house. In fact, Gemma remembered the boys in the neighborhood having to help pitch in to set fire to their nesting area in the middle of dry season when the whole pack of mongooses would stand shoulder to shoulder to do battle with other invading mobs. They would also square up against humans going about their business of working the land for their food and survival, meaning mom G and Gemma in their own yard. Those mongooses could be seen all day long if one just watched the grasses maybe one hundred feet uphill behind their house. There would be almost imperceptible movement of the grasses and occasionally a mongoose head would pop up enough to be visible. They had their lookouts posted and upon stepping out, even to go the visit the outdoor bathroom facilities during the day, their distinctive warning sounds can be heard, followed by a rush in the grass as presumably the young ones who had ventured away came back to the protection of the nest.

Then they talked about the crossing of the little ravine and then the bigger creek or river and the condition of Say-say and her home. Gemma gave a detailed rendering of where she put what inside the house and the sweeping of the yard and was rewarded with, "Thank you Gemma, you did well." Gemma's little breast was bursting with pride. Who little girl did not want to hear praise from her mommy! She outlined the discussions between Say-say, Eslyn, Randall and Margarette. Mom G listened with interest, saying very little. When Gemma told her that they had decided to 'break bush' to get to Pan-cup's house, Mom G's eyes opened wide with alarm. "What if you children got lost in that rapidly darkening cocoa?" Gemma protested, "I have been there umpteen times Mom and you know I would not have done so if I were alone." Mom G said, "I hope not girl! How many times have we heard horror stories of children disappearing never to be seen again? It's not common I admit, but I don't want it to be you my baby, ok."

Gemma continued narrating on about their trip to Mr. Pan-cup and his revelation that his name was in fact Mr. Nesbit to which mom G replied with a scoff in her voice, "How come you don't know that child? You've been going there long enough to know that. I always say, Mr. Nesbit." Gemma retorted, "Moo-am, I have never heard you say that; it's always 'Pan-cup, pan-cup'." Mom G let out a loud, "stoups" at that but didn't say more other than, "Go on now, what else?" Gemma proceeded to tell her about the remainder of their interaction. When she got to Eslyn asking Mr. Pan-cup directly if he was a dealerman, mom G gasped, "Really, she did? What a spunky child? What would she have said if he admitted to it?" At that Gemma said, "He did admit to it. He proudly admitted to dealing in cloves, spices, nutmegs, mace, breadfruit and charcoal and to therefore having a lot more money than most in the area!" Mom G slapped the table cackling with laughter and Gemma was getting concerned that the neighbors would come running at the commotion. Mom G laughing out so loud wasn't such a common thing. The poor lady had had much to bear over the years with her husband not really supporting the family financially plus having outside children while married to her and having to turn around and even work to find money to help those outside children and pay for their school fees to go to High School. Gemma reflected that those older brothers and sisters of hers, likely thought that it was money from their dad! It might have surprised them to learn that it was mom G 'busting her tail', doing whatever it took to come up with what little support she could.

Gemma then concluded the narrative about the trip back and reassured her mom G that they all had carried flashlights and those who needed it, got a big stick to help defend themselves. Mom G said, "I am proud of your friend Eslyn, that girl has some kind a gumption! And it was nice of you to volunteer to help Muriel with getting her a tin of coals so she could better help her mom. I need to try to bring some avocados for them, maybe tomorrow. I picked some today and there is callaloo too now." Gemma was glowing with the praise. So, all that was left to be done was get the dishes cleaned up and brush her teeth and think of getting to bed really. She would have washing to look forward to in the morning, then cooking and maybe baking. Hopefully she might pick up some books to read along the way. Often if she scored a book or two, she'd only have it for a day or two and mom G who was also an avid reader would try to read it too. Reading was a family affair and has been for as long as she had known herself. When she couldn't read certain big words herself, her loving brother Damian who she was fond of, would read it aloud for her and sometimes for them all too.

Gemma was now settled into bed. It being Friday night now, she could hear the expected sounds of music playing. People who had worked all week felt it was time to relax, listen to music and even dance. For some drinking was a big part of the weekend wind down. Sounds of vehicles moving back and forth had slowed and were now infrequent. All normal workers would have made it home by now she thought. The rum shops would still be doing brisk business and there were faint excited yelps as patrons who were seated inside and outside of those shops played their dominoes and card games. She could almost imagine the slaps of the thighs and the 'whack' sounds of the domino pieces hitting the boards. She could visualize the slack jawed expressions of the rum infused players, eyes hidden in dark shadows as they bent intently over their games. In her mind's eyes she could hear their shouts and waves to passing friends who called out to them but with their eyes rarely lifting off their board games would be the norm too, not even when they called out to the shop keeper, "Bring us another eight of rum over here man, we can't play without rum." Almost always, there was a low hubbub ongoing since she lived within sight and certainly within sound of the 'junction' with three popular roads meeting or depending on how one chose to think of it, starting! In the morning she thought of all the chores that awaited her and mom G. Later in the day tomorrow after those chores were completed, she would definitely want to go with mom G when she would be visiting Muriel's mom. Sleep came to her like a thief in the dark and she woke with a startle. Lifting her head off the pillow, she was barely able to see her mom's clock. Was it really 2am on that clock she thought sleepily as her mind slowly cleared?

Chapter 5.   Saturday adventures

She had had a dream, she was sure. They were a bit vague and patchy as she tried hard to bring them to the forefront of her mind. There was an overwhelming sense of feeling harried and a bit scared too. Somehow, she remembered floating through the trees in a dark forest being chased by a lady in a whitish dress. The lady had been strikingly beautiful chimera who strangely had one goat foot and one normal looking human foot. There was also an image coming to her of her reaching out to pick a lovely yellow mango hanging off a branch and as her hands got close and her fingers started to open to grasp it, discovering there was a yellow serpent with reddish eyes all wrapped around it with its forked tongue flicking back and forth. She remembered being panicked and attempting to withdraw her hand quickly only to find it happening very slowly as if her hand was embedded in thick molasses. Somehow though Mrs. Julia's face appeared on the serpent's body. She shivered in loathing and fear coursed through her body and she shifted her weight on her rough sheets. Those dreams of hers really were freaky, she thought to herself. However, she had not been falling and falling, into an endlessly black pit with no end; those were the dreams she dreaded the most. She concluded that she'd survive her brush with the chimera- part human part goat just fine, as well as the Julia-faced serpents too. After a bit of tossing and turning, Gemma must have fallen back into sleep because when she next opened her eyes, there was some pretty solid evidence of a predatory dawn creeping over the darkness and the light was winning.

Mom G stirred and was restless. It seems that her body was reminding her about all the Saturday morning chores just waiting to be done. Before too long indeed her eyes were open and she turned to look at Gemma who was wide awake and staring at her. Mom G's eyes popped open wider at that realization. Neither said anything for a while as they both gazed at the rafters which this morning did not have much moisture hanging in beads as usual. Thankfully there were no animals gazing down at them. Eventually mom G said, "You know Gemma, we have a lot to do this morning." Gemma said, "To be truthful, I can't wait. It's been a long night". Mom G said, "Are you telling me that you didn't sleep well again Gemma? Nightmares again?"
Gemma said, "I got chased by a goat-footed woman through a forest. It felt like if I let her get me, I would never be the same again. Plus, I saw the stupid scary serpent again. I was reaching for this wonderful looking ripe yellow mango, only to realize as I was about to pick it that there was a yellow serpent wrapped around it getting ready to strike out at my hand. When I tried to pull my hand back, it was like it was stuck in liquid asphalt and on top of that the serpent's face changed. It now had Ms. Julia's face. So scary and then I woke up and barely slept after that!"
She said, "As I told you, I used to have horrible dreams too. So, I do understand how scary they are. You'll grow out of them Darling. Anyway, we have lots of things to do. Breakfast has to be done, then washing, then baking and we must go to visit Muriel's mother and bring some bread to them." Gemma said, "I need to go with you Mom, to try to pick up some books to read too." Mom G said, "Ok, so let's get going out of this bed." So that's what they did.

After a quick breakfast that included some delicious bakes and a dollop of strong salty fried smoked herring with some cocoa-tea sweet with milk for mom G and lemon grass tea for Gemma with minimal sugar, it was time to tango with some large tubs of dirty clothes. Mom would take a hearty traditional breakfast when she could get it saying that it was best to start the day right. Gemma for some reason did not like thick home brewed cocoa tea with the thick skimmable layer of oil over the top of it. Mom G said that it gave her the energy boost that she needed even though it had 'heat' associated with it too. She would even enjoy it with ginger and once in a while when food or fuel was tight, she would put a few soft dumplings in it to make it into a meal. Mom G had set up the large tub. Skinny little rat that Gemma was, came from the small meals that she took. She could just about subsist on fruits and a few crumbs of bread here and there eaten on the run often. The tub was so large that one person could stay inside of the outdoor bathroom enclosure and the second person worked from the outside as it projected outside a bit. The person outside could use the wooden washing board. Simultaneously mom G has already kneaded a few pounds of white flower dough appropriately spiked with yeast and her own mix of baking powder. While they were both ploughing through the washing chores, mom G took regular breaks to check the dough and to tend the outdoor fire. Then she placed the 'tin oven' very carefully propped up on firestones over her fireplace to guard against tipping over accidents.

She told me that the entrepreneur 'Pan-cup' at one time was the only one who went to town to buy these large sheets of metal, bend, cut and shape them into those homemade ovens and more. It dawned on Gemma then as to how he made have come to be called 'Pan-cup.' This one oven was at least three years old and was showing its age. Now there were several new builders of these homemade appliances and 'Pan-cup' was all but sidelined. Too much competition and mom G said that maybe he found the charcoal business to be more profitable. Mom G had said, "Pan-cup is nobody's fool. He had spent years planting special forests of wood trees particularly suitable for making charcoal all around his property and other areas where he was allowed to. So now unlike his competitor charcoal makers, he has a ready supply of wood and makes the most solid dense good quality product. He is forward thinking." Mom G had said that authoritatively with her lip tightly pursed and nodding vigorously. It was obvious that she admired his business acumen and hardworking nature.

Gemma's backside was up in the air and her head with her skinny arms were buried down in the tub going up and down as she dipped different segments of the clothing in the soapy water, brought it up onto the juking board to work it back and forth. Once one piece of clothing was done, she dumped it into a separate little bucket the contents of which were rinsed out periodically, wrung out by hand then heaved up onto the many clotheslines strung up between the adjacent house posts or between adjacent trees like the avocado and the gospo tree. They took turns doing that hard hand numbing work. Sometimes Gemma's sister Mavis pitched in to make the chore go by faster, but not always. Gemma thought that it was a lucky thing they could only be seen by someone at their house or possibly by somebody coming down the hilly driveway connecting Mr. Renwick and their gap. The pervert Renwick or his buddies would most certainly have had a field day gawking at their rears bobbing up and down she thought. Mom G who was taller had already run a wet rag along all the clotheslines to remove crawling ants and other detritus including muck from birds and such. That was in preparation for spreading the washed clothing out to dry. So on and so forth it went and by ten am it was all done. Gemma could still hear the 'slap slap slap' of big pieces of cloth like bedsheets being banged onto the river stones by all the ladies mostly, who were just a few hundred yards away taking advantage of the free water coming from the mountains. With dry season, the water was clear and safe. That same little river often became a series of raging tumbling muddy waterfalls when it is raining up in the mountains.

Mom G's baking bread smelt heavenly too. That was confirmed when their closest neighbor popped up the twenty feet bushy track between their houses to say, "Ah smelling you bread and me stomach grumbling. Tell me when it ready so ah could come for some." No one answered; we were so busy on the washing board with the pipe running. Funny how there never was an offer to us when something nice was cooking or baking down there, yet great interest was shown in our stuff Gemma thought. It would take two turns to get all the loaves baked in the little oven even though it contained two trays and room to place some burning charcoal both on the top and bottom of the oven. Mom G was pushing hard to get it all done before the full heat of the midday sun hit. The plan was for church in the morning and therefore all major chores were to be done today. This afternoon was devoted to a walking trip up into the neighboring village of Maderville past the large estates, up toward where Muriel and Randall lived.

After the baking, it took quite a while for the bread and buns to cool down. Mom G put a few loaves wrapped in clean kitchen towels after they had cooled almost to room temperature. The rest were arranged on the little tabletop inside to cool then placed in large flat bowls covered by a large perforated basket so that they 'could air out' and not 'sweat.' They would 'mildew' if they got moist and would then be thrown out in a day in that tropical heat and humidity. Mom had Gemma run to the shop to get some 'salt meat' in the form of salt cured beef. The shops would be closed tomorrow on a Sunday. She said, "It's been long time since we made an 'oil-down'. I got a breadfruit, we have enough callaloo and a coconut so that's what we will do. Gemma said, "Mom, I hope you make a lot of it as we are sure to have people dropping in, you know." Gemma asked, "Why do people think we are well to do Mom, when a lot of those same folks actually live in nicer houses than ours, eat and dress better than we are able to? Mom G shook her head sadly while saying, "It's that damn name Crawford. They came from Scotland and there were several brothers some of whom settled in Barbados, Petit Martinique and a couple up here in the northern countryside of Camerhogne. One of their mixed sons married a Portuguese woman and your father Gilbert Crawford came out of that union. They were not poor, though definitely not wealthy. When we got married, your father always carried a suitcase full of his work, old watches that he was repairing and just lots of little parts. He operated out of a little rented shop in Granvillevale and even had a little jalopy. We his family, rarely got to ride in it though. His little 'leggobeasts' that he cavorted with, were the ones he transported in it. As a result of all of that, he's had several outside children, both before and since our marriage. Then you know the rest of the story. He killed himself with the rum. At one point, I even tried to run a little shop in addition to doing my seamstress work. So, I suppose we looked to the outside world like we were making it. Little did they know, that we have been catching our 'nennen'. After the hurricane Janet in 1955, we did not get any help because people deemed us to be too well to do. That really was just on the basis of your dad's surname you know. We ended up scavenging bits of other folks blown-down house bits to scrape together this ramshackle home we now live in. When your papa died, he left us in a ton of debt and even when he was alive, he really did not support the household at all. I still had to scrape together everything that we ate and drank and wore. Plus, I still did my best for his outside children too as you can see yourself. We have had to do without, in order to provide for his other progeny." Gemma thought about it long and hard. What was there to say?

Come midafternoon, after lunch and a cooling shower mom G and Gemma set up on their largely uphill trip. They were carrying some freshly baked bread and even two of mom G's precious avocados to Muriel's mom. Mom's avocado tree was the envy of the village, in fact several neighboring villages really. It had tremendous flavor, consistently good size and a beautiful smooth texture. It was a good substitute for meat at breakfast time eaten on a warm piece of bread. Therefore, people in the know understood that being gifted with one was not a trifling thing. So down the gravelly driveway they walked leaving Cereal tied up whimpering but with sufficient length to deter anyone from attempting to come through the front door. He had had his share of petting already after his bath in the river with its thorough rub down and getting toweled dry. So, it was time for it to do its job of being a guard dog. Out into the junction, a left turn and up Hamartan Rd saying hello to the neighbors who were out relaxing on their porches 'catching the breeze'. Then across the Guthrie bridge and through a sparsely populated area. The entrance to the Belair Estate was on the right with its tall stately palm trees along its driveway. Gemma had visited their facilities and their large covered outdoor drawers for drying nutmegs, mace, cocoa, cloves and other spices such as cinnamon was outstanding. Up the hill they went and with sparse traffic it was fun for Gemma to be doing something that felt like hiking with her mom. Something was in the air she sensed though; she could feel a throbbing, like a sound but a bit like a call. As they went further uphill, she felt the slow intrusion into her consciousness of what seemed at the root of the low-grade excitement. There was incessant drumming gradually growing, coming from over the hill. Drumming somehow had that effect on her, particularly shango drumming.

It felt like a disturbance in her inner being. It felt like something sprang into life inside of her and made her feet step in time and in tune with the rhythm. Her brain became focused on it. It was also an amazing sight to see when the Fire Baptist people came through the junction there in Zion headed for the river right near their home to carry out their rituals and offerings. Typically, they were attired in their brightly colored red headbands and white shawls moving like swirling dervishes in a dizzying blur often accompanied by an enticing array of drumming and chanting. She thought, "boy I do love the Fire Baptists and the Shango ceremonies!"

Mom G stopped to say good afternoon to a few folks who were hanging out 'taking in the breeze' as they put it in their yards. Some of them had their radios playing Sparrow, Kitchener, Calypso Rose and the fairly recently released hot 'bass man' from Shadow. Some had Bob Marley wailing away with tales of the hard life. It would have been very bad manners to rush off without inquiring about people's health and that of their family, especially those abroad. The opportunity to gossip about who was sick 'shut in' and 'on their last legs' and such, could not be passed up. Also, it informed everyone as to how prepared they needed to be for the next funeral, thus gossip was serving a very practical purpose. Sometimes it revealed that someone who had been thought to be 'at deaths door', had 'rallied' and was lately seen walking around like 'an apparition'. Mom and the gossiping friend would then nod wisely saying 'they're on their last legs anyway so this is their final hurrah!' Gemma would have to pause for the fifteen minutes that each of those conversations took and would make herself busy in whatever way she could, often playing with whichever youngsters were around. She would hear all of the stuff being discussed but would never join in 'to big people's conversation'. Doing so, apart from it being extremely boring to her, would elicit a severe reprimand from the adults. Sometimes when they spoke about really saucy stuff, they would lapse into broken French patois too. They therefore never taught the younger folks like Gemma what little patois they knew and that language was definitely dying out. Even mom G knew very little of it anyway, to hear her tell it. So, with fifteen minutes minimum for every chat, it was now a quarter to four as they reached Randall's house and his mom saw mom G from her veranda and she came plopping down her few steps to the road in her hula hoop slippers saying excitedly, "Come come Anna, it's been a while since we got to catchup with each other, what's up sister?" Gemma was a bit startled by the greeting; she always was when people called her mom by her real name Anna, Anna Crawford. She had known her mom being called by her husband's first name Gilbert for all her life, as was the custom in Camerhogne, that it therefore always caught her attention. Randall's mother Elaine and Mrs. G had been schoolmates however and related to each other in a special way. So, after the earnest hugs and sincere greetings, Gemma and her mom G were seated in the veranda with good cold lemon juice and a small slice of hard bun to cool down.

Just then Randall came traipsing in with his colorful bamboo kite on his shoulder, his ball of twine bulging partway out his pocket. He and Gemma started excitedly chattering, "So Randall, where did you go to fly your kite?" He excitedly said, "On top Mr. Charmaine's hill where he ties his cows. His son went with us and the cows know him, so they didn't give much trouble to move. Then we flew to our hearts content. It was total fun. We were up there almost all day. I did have to help Dad with some chores early this morning in the garden and after that they allowed me to go. If I had known you like kite flying, I'd have invited you, Gemma." She said, "No dice. On a Saturday morning I have way too many chores to do anything fun like that. That tells me that Good Friday will be here soon though with Carnival before it." The topic then turned to the drumming. Gemma said, "Is there a Shango close by, it sure sounds like it?" He said, "Yes. mom and dad promised to take me there at 5.30 p.m. just before it gets dark. You wanna go with us?" Gemma said, "Nothing gets inside of me as much as shango drumming you know. I can't explain it, but it affects me so much. I would love to go, if Mom G can be persuaded." He stared into the distance a bit before saying "Me too Gemma, me too, it captivates me in a way that nothing else does." Together they listened to the sinuous whine of an overhead kite that was doing a lot of dancing in the sky, though it seemed to be quite high.

Back on Mrs. Elaine's veranda, the two ladies were chatting and as Gemma and Randall approached from the rear of the house where their kitchen gardens were, they saw that Randall's Dad was walking away from the veranda. Mom G said to Gemma,

"We are going to pass by the Shango with Mr. and Mrs. Thomas with you, since I know you love that stuff, Gemma. So, when we get to Muriel's house, we can't waste any time ok." Gemma ran to her mom, gave her an unabashed hug saying, "Thank you mom and thank you Mrs. Thomas. Here I was fretting about how to persuade you to take me." Things proceeded at a brisk clip after that. Gemma and her mom left and five houses down, stopped off at Muriel's place. Muriel's mom popped her head out of her bedroom window still looking a little thin and pale to say, "Thank you, I'm feeling better and better day by day and I went to the doctor yesterday and he say ah doing much better, no infection, no complication and ah nah taking any more medicines. Ah drinking the iron tablets to build me-self back. Is me poor husband and daughter ah sorry for. Dey have to work hard." Muriel looking a little harried, suddenly perked up when she heard mom G telling her mom that they were on the way to the shango and that the Thomas's were about to join us. A little guiltily she turned to Muriel saying, "You wanna go with Mrs. G for an hour to see the shango. Ah sorry ah can't go me-self. Ah like shango so much, de drumming does speak to me heart, ah tell you." Muriel almost shouted, "Yes Mommy, thank you." Her mom said, "Well go quick and clean up yourself, you go be among decent people child. Thank you all for the good stuff you brought for me Mrs. G, ah 'appreciate it a lot." Then a male voice somewhere in the house rumbled something unintelligible and she popped her head back inside. When her head came back through the open window with a slight wincing expression on her face, she said, "Me husband say he go go too and he go take Muriel. So, they go be a little bit behind you all. You all take care you hear and be safe. Don't go into a trance and drink de goat blood ok."

Mom G. just waved her good byes and scampered down the short walkway to the road, just as Mrs. Elaine, her husband and Randall came bounding up the road. Randall was having to almost run to keep up. Shango did that to people. It called to you, it made you walk faster, you heart beat faster. Gemma thought to herself, the adults wanted badly to go to it for themselves. They're not doing it to humor us the young ones! The Thomas's were carrying a large package too. What was that about? She sidled up to Randall with her brows up and he whispered, "They want to make an offering, a contribution to Mrs. Georgi for the folks to eat who are doing the shango. That usually goes down well and gets you a better view of proceedings too." Gemma shook her head in understanding. In the past she would usually have to climb into a neighboring tree with a decent vantage point to see anything at all. As they passed the turn off to go up Pamshill leading to the slave pen and the great mountain access, there were people like them streaming down the hill to join them. A board bus trundled past as they squeezed to the edge of the roadway single file. Amazingly two goats looking out the back with the occasional bleat plus a bunch of serious faced mostly women passengers along with a few males all in white robes best she could see suggested that they too were headed to the shango. The tops of two large drums peeped out of one of the seats. This was a big deal. The pace quickened. The steady heavy heartbeat like thump thump got stronger and now as they rounded the big corner at Goodbelly hill, not only was the drumming louder, more urgent but secondary smaller drumming sounds could now be appreciated, 'Thump a baca Thump, Thump a baca Thumb,' which was even more electrifying. There was the rattle of shak-shaks, the crackling and banging from bangles, plus blowing of conch shells just not in the same manner and rhythm of the fishmongers and even the occasional sound of a ram's horn. Mom G sensing everyone's excitement, whispered to me nervously, "make sure to stay with me Gemma ok, I move you move with me, we cannot stay too long, it's easy to lose yourself in these things, remember we are observers, not real participants ok." I nodded, as I sensed her excitement but also some mixed-in unease.

People were now no longer making a pretense of their excitement, yet this mostly manifested as a strange hushed tension among the adults. Young children were blasting past them at full speed and some younger teens too. The adults despite the quickening of their steps marched on, attempting to look nonchalant and maintain some semblance of dignity. Parents were holding onto their youngsters' hands. Just a few hundred yards beyond Goodbelly hill corner, and all the folks in the procession, for that is what it amounted to, slowed down. It was a bit frightening really to approach. In addition to the heavy drums which vibrated one's insides giving rhythm to one's feet and numbing the mind, there was now to be heard as well, the crack of whips. There was the totally mesmerizing sight of the rhythmic bobbing of heads, red turbaned heads on white clad bodies moving to the drumbeat circling as if around some central object. There was rhythmic haunting chanting and even from that distance in the darkening evening, the intense concentration and sweat on the faces of those dancing could be seen. Our little family group pushed through, never stopping with Randall's father, his mother, Randall, then Mom G, myself and Muriel with her dad who had had to almost run to catch up with us now right behind. Randall and his family carried two bundles in their arms and reluctantly the crowd parted to allow them through, sensing that although they were not turbaned and robed, that they had maybe more of a right to approach than them! Or maybe it was just that Mr. Thomas was a well-known man in the area! It took about ten minutes of slog to get through the mostly silent crowd, but there was Mr. Thomas finally walking right up to Mrs. Georgi who sat red turbaned with the usual off-white dress wrapped around her, sitting in a white wicker chair and with an intricately curved stick in her hand that she rhythmically thumped onto the trampled ground in front of her. No one was smiling.

There was a young man tied with strong ropes at the neck and waist standing in the center of the circling dancers with four stern looking men holding onto the ropes five feet away from him. The dancers were going round and round in a controlled frenzied circle of maybe twenty feet in diameter. He did not look well. Sometimes folks like him were brought to Mrs. Georgi because they had medical conditions like 'fits' that the regular doctors could not seem to cure. Other times it was because they were deemed to have become possessed by evil spirits. Rumored cases of people being punished spiritually for their own or their family's wrong doing, or after an encounter with a dealer-man or mamma do-good and now needing a shango to free them, all circulated. Gemma did not know what had brought this poor young man to this juncture. He seemed wild in the eyes, trembling and occasionally made moves as if to run away. There were several maybe twenty or so folks wielding whips in an outer circle standing around the circling dancers who were cracking those whips in the air ominously as they sinuously gyrated while chanting too. It was very scary, very threatening. The drummers formed the outermost circle and there was a constant flow of assistants circulating around the seated drummers carrying small half calabash shells containing what might be water and maybe even rum too, Gemma speculated. Dancers and drummers seem to come and go from the open area underneath the house seamlessly without any breaks in cadence.

Mr. Thomas bent down and opened the paper bags containing the gifts so Mrs. Georgi could inspect and with a nod and a quick flick of her left hand a follower standing behind her reached over and relieved him of the two bags. She sat powerfully in a high-backed chair also adorned with the red turban and in a voluminous flowing white dress of thick coarse cottony material that was draped over the arms of the chair and her legs. Gemma could make out red socks and white simple shoes. There was no question that she was the one in charge of this whole shango ceremony despite her diminutive body size. Gemma was so in awe at her commanding presence. Mrs. Georgi's husband normally a wood cutter who sawed trees to make lumber, was dressed in better fashion than his usual, but still only had on dark trousers and a very old worn sort of cream-colored long-sleeved dress shirt. He was standing under their house clearly watching over the whole crowd and directing the movement of people and animals. Their house was built on pillars, high pillars with a mud floor. The yard where the dancers were circling, dancing and cracking their whips, occasionally blowing their lambi conch shells surrounded by a bevy of drummers, consisted of dry mud tamped down with a coating of dust just as that under the house too. There was a constant flow of dancers and drummers to and from the yard to the area under the house. People were being directed to tables toward food and drink which was being doled out by a few serving ladies. A few people clad in the same outfit were laying on some mats arranged side by side in a row; Gemma assumed that that meant they were catching some much-needed rest. There were bunches of newcomers who looked like those who had passed them on the bus, seated on rows of wooden benches at the far end of the area under the house. They seemed to have been ushered into the yard through some sort of back entrance and not through the front yard where the crowd was thick. Tied to several trees near to them in the yard were at least five goats and two sheep and there was an animal carcass already being cut upon hanging from its rear limbs on a nearby tree. Several very large black pots, more like vats that cane juice was boiled down in to make molasses, with actively blazing fires under them were in action and there were ladies and a few men tending them stirring their contents with long poles.

Mr. Michael, Mrs. Georgi's husband and seeming main assistant seemed to have his eyes everywhere all at once and there were five young men and women standing sternly around him, who he seemed to whisper to and they would go do his bidding. There seemed to be a row of toilets and sinks offset about fifty yards down the hill and she saw people enter and exit the lavatories, wash hands and faces before returning to their bench. Throughout all of this, Mrs. Georgia sat swaying and thumping her stick seeming to direct the starting of songs and chants. Mr. Thomas turned around and stepped aside amid the milling crowd and made his way up a slight bank. Shortly thereafter, they observed a train of people making their way, just like they had just minutes before, toward Mrs. Georgi and handing over baskets of stuff. Gemma saw several pounds of salt fish, mackerel which she could both see and smell, loaves of bread, several sticks of salami and other unidentifiable stuff that were brought and offered to her. All were accepted with a small bow followed by an imperious wave of the hand prompting an assistant to step forward, retrieve the stuff and bring it to the tables underneath the house. Such a large gathering needed to be fed.

It was now six o'clock and pretty much dark, save for the masantos being lit and a few dim electric bulbs strung on wires in several rings around the dancing circle plus underneath the house and further out. Suddenly the drummers of all the smaller instruments, blowers of horns, tambourine operators all stopped and only the big heavy drums continued. Mrs. Georgi stood up and began chanting. Gemma heard something about this 'poor soul before us who has been brought to us to have his demon removed' and a lot of other wording that sounded to her like gibberish but with the name Ashanti mentioned repeatedly. Then the ram's horn blew several times and the whips were turned onto the young man who was leashed like a dog. He was writhing and fighting but there did not seem to be any obvious marks on him, being more of a ritual beating. He went into a frenzy, alternately kneeling with his hands up in the air, seeming to speak in tongues, before prostrating himself on the ground and having 'the fits'. During this time, the full monte of musical instruments resumed with the crowd now dancing around the prostrated figure, still with his leashes on but he was no longer was being restrained by the burly men. He seemed to be unmoving now, except for obvious breathing movements of his chest. Someone sprinkled him with water while chanting incantations. Mrs. Georgi had resumed her seat. New drummers emerged for the background under the house and the prior ones slinked away with their drums. Mom G nudged Gemma after a while and said something to Randall's dad and grabbing both Muriel's hand and Gemma's accompanied by Muriel's dad, they pushed through the milling crowd. It had been an intoxicating indulgence and Gemma's feet still wanted to move with the drumming. Through the pressing throngs they went, past a line of buses, cars and motorbikes. This would have been going on for days and will likely be continuing for several more. They were now home bound with Muriel in tow. Mom had brought her small flashlight though. It was going to be an almost two mile walk back home now.

One hour plus later, after Muriel and her dad had peeled off at their gap and cautiously headed up their driveway by the light of mom G's little light, they were home, with Cereal having hysterics. Gemma let him off his leash for a while and mom G went on the little indoor kerosene stove to warm up some of the lunch meal for their dinner. They had both gone into the outdoor shower to get a quick wash up, just of hands and faces before eating. After dinner, they brushed their teeth with a cup of water and spat it out the open window. Neither of them felt like sleeping. They were still wound up by the kaleidoscope of colors, sounds, and the whole emotive experience of being that close up to a shango ceremony. This was a totally new experience to be that close to the action for both of them, thanks to Randall's dad. The excitement of the dancing swirling sweat covered participants with their flowing whitish garments swishing around them as they chanted and sang with their eyes glazed over, while simultaneously taking in the pounding drums of all types was definite overstimulation to the senses. The sight of the pugilists performing their whipping at this attempted exorcism of the young man's demon possession still was totally fresh in their minds eye. Sleep did not come until the clock showed ten pm, but they had stayed up talking, Mom and

Gemma. Neither stirred until the light of dawn penetrated the darkness of their rafters that Sunday morning.

Chapter 6.   Sunday Blessings

Then it was time to be up for church at eight in the morning. Gemma was quite relieved that there had been no scary dreams to contend with this last night. Breakfast would come after church as per custom. Teeth got brushed and water drunk, then dressing up for church was done after ablutions. Gemma regretted one thing only about yesterday Saturday. She had not been able to gather any novels at all. Surely this needed to be corrected and it would have to be done today Sunday she was thinking. She couldn't contemplate facing this whole Sunday and the week to come without some novels to gnaw on, so to speak. A person could get truly crazy from boredom she thought wryly. She lay in bed going over the wonderfully exciting and absolutely scary shango experience of the last evening. She had heard that there were times that when a goat would be sacrificed, that the dancers would actually drink the blood. Ghastly she thought, "I'm glad I didn't have to see that!" Even though she had only thought it, her face must have wrinkled in disgust. Her mom lying beside her, who she was aware of and therefore suspected she was awake, surprised her by saying softly, "Penny for your thoughts darling." Gemma startled at that. "Nothing much mom. I just thought that I was glad last night not to have to see the dancers drinking the goat blood!" Mom G chuckled, "But that's the best part you know, with it all over their mouth, dribbling down onto their chests!" Gemma jerked her head over to the left to actually look at her mom. "Are you for real mom?" Mom G burst out laughing, "I'm just kidding child. I would have been grossed out too. But I did actually see it once. It does happen as part of their ritual. I must confess though that the drumming, oh man the drumming, does get to me. I can't resist going toward the sound of the drumming! It is, how do they say, hypnotic!" Gemma simply shook her head in affirmation.

Cereal had been let off his leash to roam free as soon as they'd gone outside and he raced off after a quick nose rub into the bushes sniffing at unknown scents. He raced around the yard in circles nose to the ground, stopping to raise one of his back legs and squirt in different locations. Then he sped down the path that leads to the river. Gemma and mom G left for the little trek to church all decked out in their Sunday best. Stockings, dress shoes, long skirts and one of their better bodices. Mom G of course, had on her mandatory broach as an added touch. They met up with other church goers and even a few going to another church- the Pentecostal faith. They were headed to meet Mrs. Abrams Gemma's church nemesis, known as Mother Abrams. The wonderful lady was tall skinny white skinned silver haired and her age was indeterminate but definitely north of ninety, so everyone seemed to think anyway. Mrs. Abrams had outlived every one of her companions as well as most of her own children. Attending the Mass every Sunday and Wednesday as well as the Stations of the Cross or Novenas or whatever else was being served was a must for her. She didn't seem to get involved with the young people's stuff in the Charismatic Movement. Too much emotive and possibly enjoyable celebratory style singing and even some sort of body motion that could be construed to be dancing. Oh no, that was totally inappropriate for the elders and traditionalists in the church who if they attended stuff like that, would be only there to ensure that 'things did not get out of hand with those young people!' Then as happens with the ultra-elderly in Gemma's experience, they grow very close to their Maker. The problem was, as far as Gemma was concerned though was that she wanted, expected and in fact insisted on everyone else being as serious minded about every little ritual as she was. In that quest, Mother Abrams was aided and abetted by Mrs. Frankie which of course was the first name of her now dead husband. The reports were that she slowly became the draconian widow after the passing of her dear husband. The older folks around mom G's age were heard to gossip that it was her way of coping. Now the holy Father was her savior not just to be, but in her current life too. It had become her job to protect the Lord from noisy children who were not paying sufficient attention, and who maybe were mocking the earthly Father Mike the Lord's representative here on earth in the church building.

There was that time, yes that time never to be forgotten when pesky Gemma, trying to extract a little fun from an absolutely boring Mass as it droned on and on, had taken to watching the 'boulders' as she and friends called them and dodging them. This was of course totally logical. Who would want Father Mike's spittle to land on them? Could anyone imagine the number of germs emanating from those lips and splashing onto one's clothing, or perhaps face, God forbid, worse yet even onto one's lips. As kids, they had already been forced to sit in the first three pews. This was therefore directly under the veritable waterfall of spit, which could clearly be seen showering on the young ones with the rays of the morning sun glinting just so, through the small patches of clear glass that were a small part of the colorful picture glass windows of the church. Whoever said that the adults were dumb? They didn't want to be spat upon; they'd tell you that if, they dared to be honest. Instead, they'd say things like, "You all need to be seated where we can see and supervise you. We had had to sit in front when we were growing up too. Now it's your turn kiddos. Worse yet, could you imagine what shenanigans you little chaps could get up to, if we allowed you to sit behind us Lordy?"

So, to the front pews Gemma and company were consigned, reluctantly. Some, mostly the boys were encouraged and when that failed, forced to be the altar boys. Of course, they were at the forefront of 'taking up the collection' too. They had to carry the cross in the procession with Father Mike entering and leaving the service as well. It was all in good traditional service of course. The youngsters were already a major part of the church choir. They did have standards though. Gemma's squealing and screeching was not considered apropos for the choir, definitely. She had made sure to fail the audition. However, Darling Gemma, though not necessarily meaning to be rude or to be noticed, got noticed frequently. Mother Abrams and Mrs. Frankie both took turns in scolding her along with others too, for their rude misadventures. When Gemma's head and body would constantly writhe, dart from side to side sometimes into the laps of adjacent youngsters who sat next to her with resultant commotion among the first three pews while Father Mike was preaching, it drew their ire.

Translated it led to those two church guardians resorting to pinched ears, pinched shoulders and whatever other body part they could get ahold of. It became impossible for any of the adults sitting behind them to concentrate on the sermon. It became a genuine running battle to stifle the pestilence of Gemma and a few others when up to their antics. Those two ladies had the hardest fingers ever to be visited upon this earth Gemma could confirm. They were worse than some of the teachers.

The teachers had grown smart and would no longer brutalize their poor fingers. They resorted to giving out 'little cokes', for that was the sound made by the edge of an ordinary wooden ruler hitting kid's knuckles. If the poor student moved his or her fingers away, then you were punished with double the number of 'cokes'. So, it was better to be brave and take the number awarded you for whatever transgressions. If not, you would be made to visit the principal's office dragged along by the scruff of your shirt or bodice. Done in front of all your colleagues and getting ribbed for it later by them was no fun. At the principal's office you would be introduced to or even possibly made to be reacquainted to 'Old Huck'. Old Huck was a thick dark brown, almost black leather belt that had the reputation of being soaked in stale pee in order to keep it supple and the principal had the authority to make it go 'whop' across the back of the child who gravely misbehaved. Presumably it would straighten out kid's wayward tendencies. The few kids who seemed to not be swayed by it, were lost. They inevitably ended up in juvenile detention in Minorca and ultimately the royal jail as they grew up from a life of transgressions to a life of crime. So, no one ever wanted to go to the principal's office. The 'cokes' on the knuckles were a minor inconvenience to tolerate in comparison. Later in the day, one could also proudly display the spots of blood on one's swollen knuckles to one's colleagues anyway. It was imperative though to be out of sight of the teachers before gloating at one's bravery while crying on the inside. The ones who cried in the presence of the teachers were the 'softies'. The ones who never did get punishment were the 'goody goodies without any spunk'. Gemma though nearly at the top of her class academically was no softie nor could she be labeled a goody goody, but then again, she wasn't one of the unsalvageable rebels either. She was however an accomplished and unrepentant spit dodger.

On their way into the church while stooping to genuflect, while simultaneously making the sign of the cross, as was the correct way of showing respect and proper decorum upon entering the house of the Lord, Gemma could feel the piercing eyes of Mother Abram on her. Mother Abram 'opened the church'. She was almost always the first to arrive and would be seen saying her private prayers prior to the official start of Mass. Gemma kept her eyes on the altar as she walked straight up to the front of the church leaving her mom behind. She slipped into the right side third row where it so happened, Randall and two other young acquaintances were already seated. It was ok to walk past adults without acknowledging them in church if you did so while walking very piously hands clasped head partly bowed in respect and obviously in the correct frame of mind paying attention to the altar and only the altar. She sat down and made sure to knock Randall's knee with her own in greeting. After at least five seconds he returned the favor with his knee. It was important to wait long enough to have let the stupid adults who were watching, looking for any infraction, to have turned their gaze away from you. After ten seconds surreptitious whispering could begin, but importantly your head must stay pointed straight forward. The buggers behind would know you're talking if you inclined you head and they saw you jaw or cheeks moving. Good ventriloquism was a must in those situations. They had perfected the art of ventriloquist style talking whenever they felt it could be done undetected. Then again, it couldn't be allowed to get too loud either. There was always a conversation going on among the kids, just that they took turns. Of course, once Father Mike or whoever the guest priest was, had entered and was on the altar, there would be plans being made for the after-church activities.

Never let it be said though that the youngsters were the only ones whispering. They could hear the banter, the low murmurs and gossip going on behind them by the adults! "So and so is back with the same dress again." The answer would be whispered furiously, "Yes and all her leg is showing. Does she think this is a whorehouse?" Sometimes it was hard not to snicker. We youngsters just had to be careful. A sudden very painful wringing of one's ear could result and with no warning along with a good 'cuff' on the shoulder too if the priest's back was turned.

In a moment of reverie, Gemma remembered sitting in that same pew barely awake a couple of months ago at four in the morning on Christmas Day. In a way, it had been magical moments in a sleepy sort of way. Since she had been anticipating the Christmas morning events she had not slept well. They had gotten up, hearing the activity in and around several neighbors homes as they too stirred to make the short trek to the church. She barely remembered the walk over to be honest. The festive attitude of the people all around her was what had impacted her; certainly nothing that the priest had said could she recall.

When she had come alive was during the invigorating procession with singing down the half mile to the beach with all of the dogs of the neighborhood out barking in force at them. She made sure to tuck herself in between the throng of adults. Although it was at the dangerous hour for all kinds of evil to happen, being in a church group comprised of close to a hundred souls seemed protective. There were a smattering of torches too both electric and masanto type to afford an eerie spectacle of the ragged procession. At the beach, they waited to bear witness to the rising sun and to the scents and sounds of the bushery. Mostly there were nocturnal birds squawking at the disturbance to their routine and maybe to their nestlings. Unbothered by their group's presence, the gentle cadence of lapping waves shushed, bubbled and frothed as always, at first more heard than seen. Then with the growing light from behind the headland and seeming from under the whitish sea, the small broad line of whitecaps formed by waves breaking over the reefs became clearer to the view. There were some hymn singing and once fully bright, the procession having regrouped, headed back to the church and thence home. Christmas morning had indeed been magical. Everyone went home to enjoy a special breakfast with parang singing somewhere in the mix. Singers in trucks and other vehicles would dismount and do singing house to house, receiving edibles along the way. Gemma wished that church could be fun like that more often, but reality rudely intruded.

Anyway, Gemma survived Father Mike coming in ceremoniously marching up to the raised altar with his adult minions called deacons peeling one left and the other to the right. Gemma and mom G hadn't been surprised when Cereal had appeared by their side as soon as they'd headed down their driveway and he disappeared when they reached the church yard and they said, "Now go back home Cereal." He always returned up on time to escort them back home though, as soon as the service was finished. Gemma long suspected that he likely hung around in the area. He did this when she went to school too. Of course, church and school were yards from each other. He never seemed to get into fights with other dogs on the way there or back surprisingly. The young altar boys took up their assigned spots on either side subordinately. The service began with rousing hymns. The usual totally regimented waxing and waning of voices, songs, sing song recitations then solemn preaching punctuated with singing proceeded. Gemma did think of the cruelty of the cross and the suffering of such a well-meaning person and the sacrifice made to save the lost. The rest of the time, she rummaged through her memories of the shango yesterday and who she had to hit up for novels right as church let out.

Church was ending, meaning Father Mike and his entourage had made their exit down the central aisle toward the main entrance where he would stand just outside the front door to greet the parishioners as they left. Often, he had to rush off to say the Mass in another church though. It was now the adults to take turns to slowly crawl out. Mother Abrams was not a fast mover with her walking stick leading the way, and it was galling to have to stand there and wait. So, what happened is that there was the start of open but still somewhat hushed conversation and with major arrangements being made among the youngsters since the adults were no longer there to censor or punish. Sometimes there was still a glare or two pointed at them, if they got too loud, by the tail end of the adult procession. Therefore, they still tempered their conversation by doing a part whisper. Thus, Gemma discovered that tall skinny and very energetic Marybelle had a few detective story thrillers and Gemma could lend her a cattle-rustling western puzzler that she had in her possession. The agreed upon return day would be Tuesday afternoon at school. Marybelle would bring the books to her home around noon when she expected to be going to buy ice cubes from the shop in the junction. Randall told her that he would be passing by with his friend Alex from Standard seven a senior to them, to go to Kanhook to raid fruits close to mid-afternoon around two-thirty. They planned on staying there for one hour only, yeah, which had to be seen to be believed. Any later than that and it would be too dark down there especially if a few thick clouds covered up the sun just then. Gemma was therefore seriously tempted to go, if only she could persuade Mom G to let her go.

As they stood on the church steps, from that high vantage point, they could see much further up the hill than Gemma could from their home and even better actually than from Mr. Renwick's yard too. She poked mom G when she took a moment from shaking hands and pointing to the ridge line across the main road said, "Mom do you see how many kites are up in the air flying? Look Mom we can see all the way up the hill just above where we leave the little pasture before heading downhill into the cocoa to go to Say-say and Pan-cup. There are lines of tall palm trees both up toward Pamshill going toward Mt. Coublall and up Palmarus. There is the line of tall Mahogany, balata, cedars and poui trees. Look at all those big silk cotton trees over by the river close to our home that the serpents fly off. And Mom are those the tops of the large stinking toe vines on the trees near the edge of Kanhook?" Mom G talking excitedly said, "Oh it is a nice clear morning. Yes, you're so right child. Do you see the grugru trees in Mr. John's yard? They look like they have fruit on them now. Look, look, over there a couple of kids are doing something that I haven't seen for a long time!" Mom was giggling away. Gemma said, "So nice to see you giggle!" At that mom G said, "What you think, I'm some old dried-up old prune incapable of having fun and memories!" Gemma grabbed her Mom's arm lovingly and said, "Admit it Mom, how often do you even pay attention to stuff like that?" Gemma too had seen the kids skating down a small grassy hill, their bottoms on slippery coconut fronds.

Gemma had however, been more captivated by the more royal looking line of tall palm trees in the distance standing like policemen 'at attention'. She had always admired those exceptionally tall and stately palm trees lining the roads of those villages. She loved to hear the whoosh whoosh sound that came from whipping by those palm trees while in a bus with windows down. She had tried to run along in the roadway fast enough down here in Zion in her attempts to reproduce that effect, but only succeeded in noticing a gentle blurring of the grasses growing on the banks along the roadside. She unfortunately didn't have an engine to make the noise like the bus nor its speed, she sighed. Mom G was definitely amused and answered by making that 'rude sound' with a combination of her tongue and lips, "Stoups!" At that point Gemma said, "Mom, I thought you said, that saying 'stoups' wasn't good manners?" Mom G shook her head while giving her that special half-closed eye look as if to say, 'I give up on you, you little rascal'.

Then it was Gemma's turn to giggle as Miss Cici came bounding up like a 'jack rabbit' teeter tottering in shoes that clearly had heels too tall for her. Plus, the ground in and around the church yard was not all paved and smooth either; even an expert at wearing tall heels would probably be a bit like a drunken sailor too. "What are you two standing there giggling about?" Gemma said, "Mom saw some little boys scooting down a steep bank across the hill on some coconut branches and was so amazed at that!" Miss Cici said, "If it's those boys on the hill, it must be Marlene's, you know, the one with twelve children in the little house. They have to find ways to amuse themselves. I just hope they don't have sharp flex go up into their bottoms and balls. I heard of one child who had to go to the hospital and have surgery. People say that he couldn't have children when he de make man too." Mom G and I couldn't help but grin until it felt like our faces were about to split. Miss Cici looked puzzled at our mirth. "Wa wrong, ah didn't think what ah say was so funny." Miss Cici left us to go tackle other folks in conversation as the crowd began to thin in the church yard. "Ok ah go see you all," was her parting words as she hurried off.

As they walked out of the church yard, Gemma filled in Mom G on the day's plans when Cereal just suddenly appeared at their side, making his presence known by his cold nuzzle on their hand or leg below their skirts plus the 'thump thump' of his wagging tail hitting their legs. Once acknowledged with a gentle pat on the snout or a little pull on his ears by them both, he quietly walked along guarding his two humans. Then in a 'by the way' manner she mentioned that Randall was going to be passing by at two-thirty in the afternoon on his way to Kanhook. "Can I go with him and his friends Mom? They're only going for an hour and you know how much I love to go track down fruits." Almost surprisingly mom G said, "Yes you can go after we get the oil down cooked and if you promise to cut some broom to sweep the yard!" Trying not to sound too elated Gemma said, "Yes Mom, I will definitely cut some 'bwarbook' broom."

At home, breakfast was rustled up while simultaneously Gemma was grating the coconut for the oil-down lunch. They paused the preparation to eat briefly. Breakfast was quite good actually with mom's fresh bread baked only yesterday and fried eggs from their two laying hens that mom had spritzed a few fragments of salted codfish onto plus a few strips of sweet pepper, the kind that smells like hot pepper, while she was stirring it in the pot. There had been no need for black pepper nor added salt the way she had done her eggs, Gemma noted. It must be said that there had been a pitched battle between the hen and Gemma just to get those eggs yesterday. She had had to crawl up under the low part of the house where the hen nests, trying to avoid its sharp beak and also spiders too. Mom G had said, "Watch it with that grater, be careful to not cut up you hand girl." Gemma nodded and focused on being safe. Then Gemma cut up the callaloo that mom G had just harvested. Gemma rubbed some coconut oil on her hands first before peeling and stripping the rind off the stems. Mom G would prepare the saffron, dumplings, dasheen, breadfruit, onion, garlic pepper, chive and thyme, salt all-purpose seasoning and meat with Gemma pitching in, but after breakfast. Gemma only got to watch the main meal preparation, not to do it herself unfortunately, despite frequently asking to do so. In addition to the salted meat, a dash of stinky mackerel and salted cod fish and some chicken back and neck too all were going into the pot. So, with almost military precision, that oil-down was on the fire with bubbling banana leaves to hold in the steam in 'no time'. Mom swore that that was better than having the ordinary pot lid on with the delicious juices boiling over onto the hot coals. 'Steam comes out, juices stays in', she had repeated when I had asked her why a long time ago.

Mom G was ironing some clothes off the same fireside coals being used for the heating of her iron. There were two ancient hot irons and they both would get heated up at the same time. Then mom G would use one until it began to cool and she would quickly run outside, grab the second hot one and set the cool one back onto the hot coals. Those things were seriously hot. She would use it on the heavy coarse fabrics like thick heavy skirts and jeans type materials often turned inside out first so, as mom

G explained, they wouldn't develop an 'undesirable shine'. Then as it became cooler, she would grab into the pile for materials that 'couldn't take much heat.' Gemma had not been allowed to use the iron yet either. Mom G had to wrap the old iron in lots of rags for insulation and it really still got quite hot to handle. In between the ironing, mom G tasted the pot a few times during the cooking adding a dash more salt, before it was allowed to simmer down with the pot lid just a little askance to let out some more of the steam. Then when it was done, she picked the pot up and carried it inside to cool. They would not be subjected to the fate of a few other folks who had their whole pot of cooked food picked up and disappeared or just as bad, the poor people who lived below the road and left their pot open, only to have mischievous 'hopefully just kids' throw stones into their food.

Gemma's stomach, although she had eaten recently, did a delicious lurch at the incredible smell of the oil-down. Mom G must have noticed Gemma's reaction or she realized that her stomach also felt a little 'peck' too as she said, "As soon as it cools, I'll take out a little taste for us." What a wise Mom to have, Gemma thought, as no telling how many other folks may 'accidentally show up' just when it's time to eat. It would be nice to not have to settle for just a little taste, while watching it disappear down the throats of people who drop-in at one's table when food was being served.

After a while, mom finished her ironing, just as the galvanized roof was reaching its noisiest, creaking and popping. It was so hot that all the morning moisture had been fried off the underside of the roof she noted, looking up. She thought about the scent of mom's ironing; that mix of hot damp steamy cloth with the faintest whiff of old fried perfume fragrance, burnt starch, charcoal and hot iron with mom's face totally focused on the task. There were also the methodical rhythmic sounds made by the hot iron as it moved with a 'shush, thud, sigh, rustle and squeak' over the cloth, and as the cloth too was being moved upon the ironing table. Superimposed upon those sounds too was the varied multiple different creaks as the ironing table itself responded to the constantly changing pressure of mom G's massaging. Even the clacking sound made by the iron as she momentarily placed it on its holding stand and off again as she repositioned the fabric. She had long ago come to realize that she could deduct whether mom G was agitated, angry or calm on the inside based on the rhythm of her ironing and how gently or conversely how violently she handled the poor iron. Occasionally like after someone or something had seriously annoyed mom G, ironing sounded like the way Gemma imagined trench warfare would have sounded in World War 1 or 2, like multiple machine guns dueling to the death, to the accompanying muttered grunts 'under her breath.' She held that picture auditory, visual and odor wise in her mind's eye for a while with her eyes closed while breathing slowly in and out. That felt to her like 'home and mom' and Gemma recognized how blessed she was.

She jumped out of her reverie with the sharp rattle of the door being banged. Strange that she hadn't heard Cereal bark nor the steps creak! Could she have momentarily fallen asleep? Up she jumped like a 'jack rabbit', it could only be Marybelle. Confirmation occurred as she approached the door. Clearly visible through the open slats of the door stood Marybelle holding a bag on her left shoulder plus a plastic container in both hands and most importantly, two regular sized novels clamped under her right armpit. Gemma swiped the novel she was going to lend her from off the table as she scooted by and in a flash had the door open expecting that her visitor might want to come on in. Marybelle shook her head vigorously to the invitation of the wide-open welcoming door. "No I'm in a hurry. I've got to run before my mom break me back. The ice from the shop is soft, it already melting and Ah done pass by Janine and spent too long there. Can you slip your novel into my little 'joula bag' here please Gemma, got ta go, got ta go now." Gemma grabbed the two books and did as told saying, "Thank you and I understand girl, run run" Gemma thought of how many times she too had been in that very predicament! Marybelle was off in a flash, her bony backside bounding down the driveway. One of the two books was open and being devoured almost as soon as the door rattled shut and mom G now resting in her usual chair, fanning herself right next to the open window, had hers in the other hand. Other than the episodic fan creaking and slapping sounds wielded by her mom, plus pages being regularly turned, there was no sound being vocalized. Reading in this house of mom G was serious business.

Gemma had ripped through over one hundred pages of her soft cover between twelve -thirty and two-thirty that afternoon, when the knock rattle came. She had been warned though; Cereal must have returned from wherever dogs go for their midday break. He had dutifully wolfed down his breakfast and with relish. He had actually gotten a whole stale 'bakes' two days old, with some gravy made up by mom G consisting of scraps of mackerel, salt fish left over from the lunch preparation and a little dash of milk. He had carefully lifted the sold parts including the 'bakes' out of the slushy liquid and daintily chewed those. Then he lay down paws on either side of his bowl and hungrily lapped up the liquid part looking quite appreciative. He was a good dog, a really good dog. After his meal, with the bowl licked clean, he had come over to where we were and gave both mom G and I a cold nuzzle and rubbed his flank on our legs then went to lay down under the house.

His light brownish fur was naturally short and his whiskers which were still a bit wet got periodic swipes from his long pale pink tongue. He gave an obvious 'burp', closed his eyes to slits but not completely, breathing with those short quick jerky movements of his. His whiskers were like separate little independent creatures in their own way, twitching this way and that, accompanying his frequent nose movements as he constantly sampled the air for scents or to warn off buzzing insects. I knew that if I watched him long enough, usually from atop the stairs or from a window, if he had laid down in the shadow of the house but not directly under the house, the next step would be a change in his breathing pattern to slower shallow breaths and a transition to twitching of more than the whiskers on his long blackish snout. His legs would be the next part of him to start twitching. He would obviously be dreaming. He did that after a good meal in the daytime, when he knew we were safe and in-house. If we were down on the ground as we were then, the huge guard dog in him wouldn't allow him to go fully to sleep. At night he didn't seem to sleep much at all, as his huffing at the slightest disturbance and the slight rattle of his chain would be evident anytime that I came awake. So, he got to sleep, eat and 'dreevay' during the day especially on a weekend. Of course, his self-imposed duty to take Gemma to and from school or to wait by the roadside with anyone who was looking to 'catch' a bus was all part of his self-imposed duties too.

Gemma heard the informative but questioning 'woof' cough-like come out of Cereal's snout. She thought, "Has to be Randall and the bugger is right on time. Not bad for a kiddo. I wonder what he will become later in life. He sure is punctual." She wondered, "Heck, I wonder what will be my fate too, apart from the inevitable death which will get all of us eventually?" All the while she was reluctantly setting aside her novel with a glance at the page number and she quickly stuck a pencil that was close at hand in between the pages. Then she relented and stuck in a used envelope instead. It was not her book, and it would be unsightly to leave a pencil to deform its otherwise 'newish' appearance. Her mom had instilled in her the principle of returning borrowed items especially books, in perfect condition. She had come to realize that some of her friends did not take such good care and had earned, appropriately a bad reputation to the point where they could not be part of the book borrowing circuit anymore. She did not ever want to land in that nasty pot. By the time she had opened the door to see Cereal wagging his tail but still standing at a distance from the two, Randall and Alex as he had promised, were just feet from the door steps. Randall proffered a plastic shopping bag with quite a few french cashews plus many other fruits in it and said, "These are from my neighbors for you and Mom G. My parents told me to pass on their regards." Gemma reached out and took the bag, walked back inside and emptied its contents over by the sink letting mom G know that the boys were here and of their greetings. Mom G lifted her head from her book barely, peering over her reading glasses for only one second, if that. With the slightest tinge of annoyance, she said, "Don't forget my broom and take our cutlass. I got Mr. James over at the boxing plant to sharpen it a few days ago on the grinding wheel. So, it is very sharp, don't cut yourself. You know how hard it is to cut boisbook!"

Chapter 7.   The Boisbook campaign

Gemma was already dressed with long pants and had stepped out through the door onto the landing at the top of the stairs since

Randall and Alex had retreated down onto the grassy yard. "Before we go down to Kanhook, do you mind making a quick run up the hill to 'Poland' with me to get some broom for Mom G?" Randall nodded and Alex said, "Oh Lard oh, Ah glad you said that, 'cause ah need to get three set ah broom too." Even 'Mouse' as Randall is called piped up, "You're right, me mommy will be happy for some too." They each had cutlasses and as Gemma stepped out with some twine and a large fine bag, Alex said, "Wa you need de bag for girl?" Gemma answered, "The bush is like wire when it rubs on me and I need to get not just for us, but for me neighbor too. If I get only for us, she will simply come under the house and "borrow" ours, like forever borrow." Alex gave his odd belly laugh and pointing to the various neighbors' houses asked, "Which one?" When his finger pointed to Ms. Cici's, Gemma nodded. He said, "Ah ha some neighbors just like that too. In fact, ah have the same reasoning like you. Bring it to them, so they doh come get yours." He belly laughed again in that rather odd way of his. She had heard that although he had not passed his common entrance exam in Standard five and therefore was going to have to do the school leaving exam so that he could have a piece of paper to his name, he was otherwise brilliant and was an excellent budding carpenter. In fact, she had heard that he could do almost anything that involved construction type work. "Appearances could be deceiving, including how one spoke," she thought silently to herself.

They hustled off, across the road, up the barely discernible trail on the side of ole Maze's house, scrambling past some big stones that were stained with 'lallee' and moss. Cereal was with them, his nose an inch behind Gemma's heel. Not more than five mins later they were wending their way between smaller boulders and onto scrappy grass interspersed with thigh high shrubbery. Someone, Gemma couldn't remember who, had told her that the combination of grazing sheep and poor-quality soil between lots of stones, led to this place being ideal for the growth of only hardy bushes and shrubs. It appears that nobody worked this land and the true owners were likely abroad anyway. The rough shrubbery grabbed at Gemma's pants legs and she was grateful that her thighs were thus covered. They were fragrant in a manner of speaking 'bush-wise' though not the wearable fragrance type. Alex said, "Come over here, that's some good bwarbook right deh." With that, cutlasses started to swing with thuds, whereas Gemma's went 'swish swash'. After she had cut enough, she looked up to the realization that there were no cutting sounds from the others. Alex stood there with his cutlass stuck in the hard ground where he had impaled it and was waiting patiently. He said, "Man dah bwarbook real hard an ah see how you cutlass cutting through it like butter, so ah waiting to borrow yours." Gemma handed it over to him and said, "Just don't dull me cutlass you hear!" She was giggling inwardly as she said it, partly in amazement that with so little time spent in Alex's company, she was already adopting his style of speaking in broken English which truthfully was how most of the kids and even adults of the village really spoke. Mom G would 'bust her tail' though for speaking in the ordinary vernacular around her. "How you going to get a respectable job in life if you don't speak correctly eh? When you go to town and you hear the professionals talk whether in the bank, the hospital or on the radio, how do they speak?" That was the admonishing she would get from her mom G and even her Godfather Dr. Benny. Of course, she could speak as 'bad' as everyone else did, as long as it was out of earshot of those speech police. That included her teachers too, for the most part. Of course, she had overheard the teachers speaking in the worse possible broken english among themselves. Some of them even knew a few French patois words too. 'Do as I say, not as I do' was a common imposition in life she had long ago already learned.

Anyway, the broom branches were sorted by length and robustness and tied together in little sweep sized bundles. The very short stemmed ones were to be tied to long sticks carefully for use on cobwebbing duty. The really long stemmed ones were best for doing the main yard sweeping so that the adults didn't have to bend their backs too much. The shorter ones were for use in confines spaces, like under the house, as most houses were built on stilts and had an open area underneath. The now completed brooms were placed inside the bag in Gemma's case or otherwise lugged by hand down the hill. Gemma dropped off a broom to Ms. Cici who said, "Thank you, but you only brought me one." Gemma who knew her neighbor well had been surprised to hear the thank you, but not at all taken aback by the criticism and so she was already running up the bank that separated their two yards when the remark came, thus obviating the need to reply. Even long after the leaves had fallen off, the branches would remain tough, resilient and wiry and could keep going as an effective broom for many weeks.

Gemma on the way back, had told Randall that there was a medium sized soursop almost ready for him to take to his parents to make soursop ice cream sometime in the coming week when it ripened. Literally with some added rum, and not any old rum, but with River Antoine rum added, even just a 'smidge' that sour sop ice cream would become irresistible. In fact, Gemma truly believed that if heaven did not have River Antoine spiked soursop ice cream, it would not be worth going there. Mom G knew that to be a favorite of her friend, Randall's mom.

Mom G lived on a very small plot of sloping land. At the top of it was the hilly bank which bordered Mr. Renwick's, from whom they had purchased it anyway, after years of renting the same lot. That escarpment and its surroundings was the no man's land where the mongooses had tunneled multiple burrows into the cliff. There was a shifting battle-front up there. The mongoose colony would go through periods of increased viciousness, likely when mating and having young. Those seemed to be the times that anyone, man, dog, or fowl, as in chicken, would be under threat by vicious possibly even rabid looking animals charging toward them almost to the walls of the house itself. Going to the outdoor latrine became a dangerous thing necessitating having a long stick for one's protection. Going to that topside garden was an invitation to have a line of head bobbing animals standing on their hind legs hissing and charging in a very threatening way. Sometimes there seemed to be pitched battles going on between them and other invading mongooses and it was possible to open the back wooden windows and look out at the weeds rustling, swaying amidst vicious sounding hisses and catch glimpses of the entwined animals tumbling around. Sometimes mischievous boys came by to set traps and take them away. Mom G and I didn't really want to know what happened to them. We did hear though that they were killed, and their heads sent off to get their brains analyzed for rabies. That was part of the regular government surveillance for rabies within the mongoose population. There must be some payment for those little rat eater brains obviously, from some government agency. They did hear that some particularly cruel boys set fire to them just to watch them run around 'like crazy'. Reportedly, someone's house very nearly got burnt down that way, which stopped the practice locally anyway. That kind of cruelty was hard, very hard to stomach, Gemma thought.

Anyway, on mom G's small plot, she had assiduously nurtured some key trees. She had a very tasty well known breadfruit tree, an avocado, a citrus gospo tree, a plantain stool that people usually stole whenever it bore fruit and lots of callaloo. She had a small drainage area that stayed wet even in dry season which was used for regular dasheen bush callaloo as was in the oil-down being cooked. There was also lots of zeppina or Jamaican callaloo growing wild around the yard, which they used to cut like it was a weed before learning its value a couple of years ago. Then close to the drain were several stools of dasheen and tania used for its tuber as 'provision' full of delicious carbohydrates to cook with meat, rice, beans like a staple. When Gemma asked her parents and close friends as to why those root crops were called 'provisions', she was rewarded with blank stares. "They are called provisions because that's what they are," she was told. It was Dr. Benny who suggested that in the days of sailing ships putting into port, before refrigeration of course, they would take on water in barrels and provisions. Those would be good items that could last the weeks and months to feed the crew and passengers. Root tubers like cassava, sweet potatoes, yams, dasheen, tania could last that long when stored properly. That was his belief anyway and Gemma adopted it since 'it made sense'. There had been one solo dwarf coconut tree on the back side of the house that occasionally would provide a 'jelly' or two for drinking its cooling water and soft fleshy coconut meat within for slurping up.

Also, on the topside bank would be where they had to risk life and limb to compete for territory to plant pigeon peas, beans, yams that seemed to thrive almost at the mouth of the mongooses' dens. 'Ah but life is tough', Gemma thought. In and between Gemma utilized every possible space to grow her favorite, cucumbers. Mom G also tried to grow her pumpkins and had had lots of success with them, much to Gemma's dismay. Somewhere, somehow, years ago her loving brother had conjured up some exceedingly nasty stories to tell her around lunch time about yellow diarrhea for the sole purpose of turning her off pumpkin soup, so that he could 'help her by taking her portion too'. Well they, meaning her much older brother and sister too, had been successful beyond their wildest dreams. So, whenever mom G made her super delicious nourishing pumpkin soup, Gemma would push it away after scarfing out the yams, dumplings or whatever could be removed and eaten by itself separate from the soup. Her older heartless siblings could count on getting double share if that soup was part of the meal. Gemma had to do without. Another reason that she grew like a bean stalk, apart from her father's genes of course.

Chapter 8.   Off to Kanhook

Off they went to Kanhook, Alex, Randall and Gemma after the broom harvesting. This time all three had bags and the boys kept their cutlasses. Gemma left both her mom's sharp cutlass and protesting Cereal behind. They took the roundabout scenic route, all the more opportunities to detect and plunder the obvious as well as hidden resources. They swung wide on the edge of Kanhook, passing by Mrs. Baby Dug. She was the only one with a tonkabean tree in the area and every now and again, there might be a few loose ones to be had and she would be nice enough to donate. They were prized for baking although mom G said that like the flesh of the nutmeg seed, it was quite poisonous and must be used sparingly. She had some hillside lands where she grew manioc (cassava) both the sweet and bitter forms and also had much prized delicious and very stomach-filling mamie apples. Mrs. Baby Dug also had the softest, sweetest sugarcane which was locally referred to as crayfish cane. It was sort of reddish with yellow bands of color arranged in spirals around the long-segmented juicy sugar filled stem segments. After a good soursop ice cream, crayfish sugarcane was next in line as a delicacy for most people. Gemma specifically had her own unique preference list though. For her the epitome of a tasty treat was the sugar apple, white fleshed with a unique mixture of smooth as well as sweet granular textured fleshy bits surrounding black elongated seeds. There it was, the secret of the visit to Mrs. Baby Dug revolved around sugar apples at least in

Gemma's hopeful head. So, Gemma had come with her bag containing what mom G had said that Mrs. Baby Dug liked. A soursop and especially three of mom G's precious avocados would do the trick. Mrs. Baby Dug from experience would be thrilled by those gifts and would then typically reciprocate joyfully.

"Good evening Mrs. Baby Dug," Gemma called out from the road near to her 'gap'. Unlike lots of other people who had nicknames, she was fine with being called that. In fact, even though mom G might know her real name, Gemma did not, nor did the boys either when she asked them as they'd gotten closer. There were two very good reasons to call. She had two very big dogs that were known to be bad tempered as she too reportedly could be also. 'Like dog, like master' it has been said. Gemma hadn't seen that side of her to be honest. She saw her as a tall super skinny very dark-skinned lady in her seventies or early eighties who had a very deliberate foot dragging walk, and a unique clarinet-like fine voice. Her head was always tied with a colorful often red cloth scarf with strands of grey peeking out along the edges. The answer came from inside her house, "Yes I'm home. Is that you little Gemma? Come, come, the dogs won't bother you all." As if on cue, her 'horses' started to bark. Those dogs reached up to Gemma's chest and made Cereal look like a little mutt, which truthfully, he was! They sounded like they were tied way to the back of the yard.

Gemma stepped up off the road over the raised culvert and up the walkway toward the house. At the base of her stairs, she lifted her head up to see Mrs. Baby Dug emerging from her creaky door shuffling forward with her trademark gait. Her eyes pinned Randall and she said, "You look like Elaine Thomas's boy, you look 'pit Elaine'." Randall said, "Good afternoon Mrs. Baby Dug. Yes, I am Elaine's son Ma'am. My mom always mentions you. She always says that you are a cousin." At that Alex piped up with his own greeting too. That was a good thing. Right after that Gemma immediately stepped in to say, "My mom sent you some large avocados and a soursop too." Mrs. Baby Dug's eyes gleamed with pleasure as she said, "Oh my, you mommy is a good woman. I am very grateful for the avocados in particular. Her avocados are out of this world, so starchy, so sweet. I love to put a slice of it between my bread or bakes. Ah

doh ha no need for meat when I have her avocados Lordy."
Gemma concurred with that opinion, since she too liked her
avocado on bread. She was however more excited at that
moment, at how all three of them had coordinated by accident
more than anything else, to guide Mrs. Baby Dug's thoughts
away from what would have been an extensive diatribe on how
she and Randall's mom Elaine came to be cousins and whether it
was as first, second or third. That had been nice; like a one, two,
three punch to keep her from even launching. They had 'dodged
that bullet' was the term Gemma had read in books that would
apply here.

Mrs. Baby Dug had retreated into her house with Gemma's bag
and they could hear her muttering inside. When she returned
with the bag, it certainly had contained within more stuff than it
had going in. Gemma who was at the top of the stairs received it
with thanks. Mrs. Baby Dug said, "Take this home to your Mom
G please child. Tell her 'thanks a million for what she sent. God
go bless ha. Ah put some tanka bean, cassava with some farine,
some black sage for her to make tea, bread-nuts, two sapotes,
sugar apples but they not ripe yet and you all could go round
back and grab a mamie apple each too." Music to our ears is
what each of us were thinking while trying not to have our faces
split wide open with grins. Three "Thank you Mrs. Baby Dug"
rang out and they wasted no time following her directive. Then
armed with delicious mamie apples, one each, they came back to
the front porch and seeing that she was inside, beat a hasty but
polite retreat. They did turn and wave at her front door while
shouting, "Thank you and have a good evening". Back in the
main road, springs in their steps, they forced themselves to walk
slowly while they thought she had a chance to observe them.
Once around the corner though, they high-fived and raced down
the street with glee. Randall had volunteered to carry Gemma's
mamie apple since her bag already had a lot of goodies and the
heavy fruit would likely have crushed the other stuff in there.
Gemma's admonishment to him with a grin was, "Make sure you
hand over mine when we get home!"

Kanhook was directly ahead. Some said that some of it was
owned by private individuals whose families simply neglected it.
Others said that it was 'crown lands' that during the war,
meaning the Second World War, people were offered the

opportunity to go in there and plant their gardens for their survival. That was a time when ships could not come and go safely since the German U- boats could and did torpedo them with terrible loss of life and goods. So, it was up to everyone to produce enough for the population to survive and to perhaps help with provisioning visiting warships too. Thus, there became a culture of planting in some of these crown lands. No surprise therefore that after 1945 the remnants of some of those plantings remained wild in those places. It meant that there were myriad numbers of fruit trees, dasheen and other such ground tubers gone wild and still thriving in areas where the sun still managed to shine like next to river banks. Maybe some people still snuck in to plant and harvest too. Definitely many in the village still went in there to reap, the three of them were proof of that. So, the woods of Kanhook were riddled with trails. To Gemma and her friends, it could have been two hundred acres. In truth it was more likely twenty to thirty. The tall wild trees, the river with a few minor creeks draining into it, the rich and varied topography which insulated large parts of it from the sound of traffic all conspired to make it seem huge, mysterious and certainly even a bit dangerous. It was a place where a little boy or girl would not want to go by himself or herself certainly. Hence it made sense to tackle it in a pack, a trusted pack too.

Mr. 'Brave' Randall, since he acted that way by taking the lead, brought them to the edge of a little clearing after taking a few winding, very dark trails. The darkness had been pressing in on them, thick humid tropical moisture infused with the scent of damp rotting vegetation clawing its way down their throats. Moving that fast, left them no choice but to breathe it in. There was sudden lightness as they clambered up between some thick dark brown snake-like roots. It was a clearing with new growth. One huge tree had fallen there taking a few smaller ones with it and the sun dappled land was growing wild with a tangle of rough young grasses and low-level saplings. Among them were a few papaya trees, guava, french cashews, regular cashew nut trees and Pommerose trees too. Gemma thought that whereas some may have been deliberately seeded by humans, it was likely that most came there by bird droppings. They had to compete with lots of birds, squawking and flapping. In fact, many of the best looking and very ripe fruit already had bird 'jukes' on them. There had been many human visitors there, as evidenced by multiple hacked out trails through what would otherwise have been a very dense tangle of razor grass and bramble. The rod that they had carried and left by the roadside when they went to Ms. Baby Dug came in handy now. It was short, but by climbing at least partway up some of the fruit trees, they were thus able to reach 'a ton' of fruits. Their hands were sticky especially after the fleshy portion of the cashew nuts, but they were careful to save the nuts for later roasting. Gemma took particularly special care to not touch her clothes. The juice stained things permanently, she knew from experience.

There was an urgent need to get back, so they had decided to forgo any further exploration. Heading back toward the river, they slipped over the roots of a jumbie bead tree and some stately mahoe. Gemma could swear that she passed close to where there must have been a donkey eye vines too, since she saw a few degraded pods. She thought to herself 'this is a spot we need to remember'. Donkey eye seeds were fun, sort of. One would mischievously rub the seeds vigorously on a hard surface which would make them blazing hot and entice some poor unsuspecting underclass young man to touch it lightly. Serious and rather creative yarns had to be made up to get the poor soul to touch it lightly and briefly. Then all the knowing students standing around, would erupt in wicked laughter. High points would be given for inventiveness of the story and how effective it was. People at least made a good attempt to not have the tricked one to hold it any longer than a fraction of a second. Another fool now initiated was the rationale, but there were serious burns to be had if the ruse was not conducted well. Ah well, 'what is a joke for schoolchildren was likely death for crappo', referring to the nasty games that youngsters played with toads often resulting in their non-survival. The irony was that Gemma had learned that in some islands with strong French heritages, those same toads were a delicacy called mountain chicken. If Mr. Branson her neighbor learned of that she mused, then woe-be-onto all the 'crappos' in the area!

Close to the river now, Gemma saw evidence of armadillos rooting, what most called 'tattoo' and she was sure that there would have to be lots of manicou (opossum though a very fast moving variety) feeding around the area too. If only Mr. Branson her neighbor got wind of this, he'd be down here in a flash with his dogs. There was sure to be a lot of lajabless, ligarroo, jumble, soucouyant with visiting obeah men and women coming to cut deals with the devil between the roots of the silk cotton trees here too, if one were to be stupid enough to stay here any later. Alex, who had a watch amazingly, said, "Gotta go, it getting dark, is after five now. Ah doh wah lajabless to blow in me face you know. Leh we go quick quick you hear." Exactly what she was thinking, Gemma thought. Randall, didn't say anything, but they all picked up the pace. On the edge of the river, they looked for a shallow section to cross over stones so as to not to have to get their feet wet and they happened upon a few caccoli trees meanwhile. They grabbed a few of it's bean like fruit, those that had the beginning of a yellow tinge to them and kept on going.

Finally, they got to crossing and on the next side pulled themselves up the bank by grabbing onto some branches. Too late, they realized that their hands would now be stink from the glorisita scent. Gemma thought 'oh no, now I have to wait until I get home to resume eating!' They ended up walking through some cocoa, spice and nutmeg trees that was obviously part of someone's cultivation. Gemma was hoping that it wasn't someone who had set up man traps to catch thieves. Then she realized that they were on the back end of Mr. Renwick's farm though not where his evil 'bull-cow' roamed. She gleefully piped up, "I know exactly where we are now. We are a hop skip and a jump from my home, follow me boys." With that she took the lead and the young men who were as eager as she was to get back to civilization, did as commanded. One more crossing over the river and they were looking up the hill at Mom G's house a few hundred feet away.

First things first Gemma thought, 'get my mamie apple'. That she did, retrieving it from Randall's bag. They greeted mom G who had been sitting inside peering out the window, catching some cooler air. Then they spread out their loot from the clearing in the forest and divided it equally. Gemma was generous to give up one or two tanka beans to the boys to bring home to their moms. They made plans to follow the river down to the waterwheel at the River Antoine rum factory and thence all the way to the estuary where the river and the sea met at Potry beach. That would be a real adventure. Gemma remembered previous forays like that with great fondness. There had been lots of caccoli and its bigger fleshier version puadoo to suck along the way then. They could even combine it with some fishing for crayfish too. They all went to the outdoor shower and soaped down their sticky stinky hands and Gemma got the soursop that had been promised for Randall. He could finish its ripening process at his own home.

Their little group briefly discussed the upcoming Carnival Season. Unfortunately, not very much happened in their village in relation to the carnival celebrations. One had to go to Granvillevale to really see decent Wild Indian bands performing, or to get scared by the Short Knees with their powder spraying, Jab Jabs with their demonic horns, helmets chains, blood red lips and large hopefully defanged serpents. There were the more benign raconteurs who for a fee, would recite amazingly long threads of history detailing the exploits of Sir Francis Drake or other such historical figures and the role they played in these parts. Other individual mass players would have little boxes filled often with dirty little peep shows featuring dolls or wax figurines that one could glimpse for a small fee, while they sang interesting though mostly 'dirty calypsos'. They agreed that they were unlikely to be allowed to go together to the big towns to partake until they got to be much older and so they had to just 'chill' and get a glimpse of whatever might pass through.

Off the boys went hurrying to get home before it turned 'pitch black'. Gemma hurriedly brought her loot inside to show Mom G what Ms. Baby Dug had sent for her as well as what they had scrounged up from Kanhook. Mom was smiling and happy to get some tanka bean and farine too. She liked to put some farine in her morning hot cocoa tea to thicken it, she would say. She often claimed that it would 'keep her stomach good all day'. She also was enthusiastic watching as Gemma displayed her haul of fruits. She said, "You just about have enough cashew nuts now, when these get dried out, to make a decent parching. You may get to eat a good number of cashews. Just remember to do it when I'm here to help you. The oil explodes out of those flying cashews and will burn you up something terrible." Gemma nodded gratefully.

Chapter 9.   Easter is here with trouble

Good Friday came and went with its cacophony of dueling kites in the sky. The informal competition between mostly boys and men, for the loudest, the highest flying, the prettiest, most intricate designs and all that went on. Of course, there were few high hills that were bare and windy enough for kite flying. Trees and buildings were the places that kites were not allowed to go. Only death and destruction awaited the poor unfortunate ones which got entangled. It all meant that kite fliers got bunched together all flying from the same hills and thus arose the razor blade kite tails. Expert maneuvering by some kite fliers to swish their kite tails across the twine of others led to a 'cutting' which would lead to a chase to retrieve it. The chase would be both by the owner and others who often would assert 'finders are keepers' rights. Particularly if a kite was very desirable, owners may get involved in disputes both verbal and with fists. So, no wonder that kite flying season was rife with hordes of youths racing through villages yelling 'it caput and 'kite cut, kite cut' and interesting confrontations too. In the midst of all that, Gemma calmly made her weekly trips to bring mom G's gifts to the underprivileged, getting regaled with stimulating stories of mythical creatures and sometimes dissections of the family tree of prominent villagers. It formed a good break from the humdrum of her daily life anyway. Along the way, she foraged for the things of real value in her life, fruits and books to read. After that Easter Sunday celebrations were a big deal with Mom G making a big effort to put out a nice Sunday meal.

It was a time of growing turmoil in the small country with brewing talk of general strikes by trade unions. There were scattered skirmishes between a new political party over beach access rights for the general public and since those events were the talk of the village, Gemma overheard whispered talk among the adults almost everywhere she went. She even caught a glimpse of a secretly circulated newspaper, very roughly printed, making the rounds of the village. There were breathless rumors being circulated and discussed in soft whispers, even among the rum drinkers in the shops and everywhere as to who supports who politically. On the radio, ominous government sponsored special newscasts about certain rogue elements in society fomenting trouble became a frequent troubling occurrence. There was an undercurrent of excitement, like when carnival was near but different because there seemed to be a hefty dose of brewing conflict.

Anyway, Gemma's life at school continued mostly unperturbed with the excitement of herself, Randall and a few others tramping through the Kanhook forest and occasionally even meeting other neighborhood kids doing the same. There would be fun and greetings, excited exchanges of information on good places to hunt for different fruits. Visits to the older folks to deliver care packages continued without fail too; mostly Gemma had lots of company now to accompany her on those trips.

Chapter 10.   Bushery trek

One notable weekend they decided to walk and hike in and along the river that passes through the village and follow it all the way to the sea via the rum distillery. Alex had told them that he knew the whole route, having gone with some older boys in the village. Gemma recalled that her older sister and brother had done trips like that before, but she as a much smaller child had never been welcome to tag along. They were seven to ten years older and told her point blank that she couldn't go where they and their fellow teens we're headed. As much as it was true, it had been a sore point with poor little Gemma. It was even more hurtful to be constantly be called by her older sister 'mistake'. Mostly she had grown up feeling like one really, at least where they were concerned to be honest. Although she tried to be nice and helpful to her big sister, she never felt much appreciated though. Anyway, she now had her friends with whom she could explore and have fun and no chance was wasted. After a bit more than half a mile, which seemed to take ages to do, alternately jumping from one river stone to another, other times walking through the shallow areas and occasionally resorting to trudging through the tall weeds on the river bank, they began to hear the sound of water falling. Alex excitedly said, "That's it. We are going to be on top the water wheel soon."

It was indeed exciting. The river water was channeled and diverted over a big hill it seemed to Gemma, whose legs were shaking just looking down. The water rushed down the man-made channel and was falling onto a very large slowly spinning slatted wooden wheel where it was being caught in what seemed like buckets attached to the wheel. It seemed to Gemma that they were thirty feet at least up above where the water splashed out of the bucket like Santa sleighs on the wheel back into a channel where it seemed to rejoin the river. Alex skidded down the trough carrying the water to the top of the wheel, jumping off to the side and out of the water just before he could be dragged into the rotating water wheel. Not wanting to miss out on the adventure, but with her knees shaking, Gemma followed the group. She only did it once though. Feeling very lucky to not have fallen into the bucket, dragged in by the force of the water, she contented herself with only one round. She happily watched the boys do it over and over. Alex had told them that the workers of the factory did not like kids doing that. Being a Saturday, there seemed to be no one in sight down below among the big ramshackle buildings with rusted galvanized tin roofs. Nevertheless, fragrant smoke constantly oozing out of about four chimneys tinged with the scent of molasses and the heavy almost intoxicating odor of good quality rum said that there must be human activity within. This was the good premium River Antoine rum, the kind that her dad and his buddies rarely could afford to drink Gemma thought, remembering having to see him imbibing even at lunchtime when he took a break from fixing people's watches. She shivered in disgust at those memories of having to help drag him out of drains that he fell into on the way home and she, a tiny little girl trying to pull him out as best she could with the worst, most unmentionable curse words blasting out of his mouth. She quickly shifted her mind back to the next task at hand. "How are we going to get out of here?" She said in her mind.

Well, Alex and Randall had a plan. They weren't going to jump on the wheel and ride it to the bottom. They trudged back along the channel up and away from the distillery, rejoined the main river and carefully followed it as before. Part in and part out of the water. Having bypassed the plant, they paused to look back up at the huge ancient weather-beaten water wheel with amazement at the thought that they had been 'all the way up there'. They resumed their trek down river passing over some sections that must have been particularly popular with the folks in the area for washing. The stones here were very smooth and covered with that permanent whitish sheen that comes from soap and soap scum. Gemma and the group were experienced river stone walkers and jumpers, but along that patch of the river, they found themselves having to take extra care not to slip off. They each knew of kids and adults who had broken bones after slipping and falling under similar circumstances. There were even a few ladies washing who looked at them bug eyed when they saw them approaching. The eye message was 'don't you kids walk anywhere near my already washed clothes or else'. Gemma and the crew took to the banks and politely nodded, waved and said good morning as they passed. The hard looks previously directed their way softened as the ladies said, "Way you all going children, ah hope you all steer clear of the bushery. Ah doh want you all to go walk in de dirty water down there and get worms up inside you foot. Sore foot eh good you know. And watch it on the beach too. Way the river meet de sea, there does be strong current you know dah go drown you. So doh go in the water on dah beach. Too many people drown down dey ok." We nodded gratefully and Alex said, "Thank you ma'am, we doh plan to bathe today on de beach. Have a good day."

They could smell it. Salty, with that special seaweed-tinged odor; the beach with the wide flattened river mouth full of meandering pools of dark tannin-stained water with mangrove standing on tiptoes nearby. They had noticed that the river had widened and was flowing more slowly. On the right side bank was cane, yes fields of it. It made sense as it was in proximity to the distillery and sugar mill. All of this area was once full of sugarcane harking back to the days when sugar was king in these former British islands. Now, in the smaller islands, Gemma had been taught sugar had to be imported from the larger islands where there was more flat land and all the phases of planting, harvesting and production of molasses and various grades of refined sugar from cane was more mechanized and ultimately cheaper. Thus, sugarcane was now a shadow of its former self. Even molasses, the main raw material used to make the artisanal rum at this River Antoine distillery was mostly imported from other big islands nearby she had been told. It seemed a bit sad and depressing, but then again, she had learned how terribly hard and back breaking it used to be for cane workers when it had been manual labor by man and donkeys. On their left bank, there were bananas in neat rows for as far as her eyes could see. They trudged on with quickened step along the banks that were now marked by raised almost black clumps of mud. Gemma could almost imagine some large mythical beast depositing those and especially so as the scent grew more and more earthy. The red crabs guarding holes next to the piles of wet looking mud that scurried away with a flurry of scraping sounds told the story though. Occasionally there would be a plop sound as the crustaceans disappeared down water filled holes. They all now watched their steps carefully. Breaking a leg down inside of a crab hole was not nice, definitely not nice she thought.

Up by her house and further up toward the mountains, along creeks, rivers and swampy areas, there were crab holes to be found yes, but they looked different. They were called land-crabs by everyone. They were cream colored, well known for dragging all kinds of fruit into and around their burrows, even nutmegs and the red lacy mace draped over the seed. Down here the sea crabs looked different. They were reddish pink and some were blue tinged and they were plentiful. It was now a matter of where there wasn't a crab hole, fresh or old. Picking one's steps was now much more arduous and the mud excavated by the crabs was wetter and more stinky. Furthermore, the river had spread out so wide and shallow with dark stained water plus what seemed like a dark impenetrable forest of mostly mangroves, so now their only alternative was to cast a wide berth and walk between the banana plants heading toward the distant sound of breaking waves. Even here the crabs were doing a brisk business of churning up the dark wet sucking mud that was getting into Gemma's poonkasol. Those were her cheap little canvass perforated shoes which let in everything from mud to stones and definitely water. It did mean that they were invading somebody's private land though, so they made sure to walk even faster and not to look too hard at the occasional bunch of ripe bananas hanging off the trees. There was no profit in being accused of praedial larceny for taking a shortcut to the beach from the river.

They'd moved through the bananas and were now among stands of coconut trees swaying gently in the sea breeze. They heard some children playing and saw some scraggly kids, some naked and a few with what once may have been underwear now hanging like grey cords around their parts. They waved to them and scooted past. Sand, clean looking sand greeted them with waves rolling in daintily and breaking into long rows of gentle white surf in unruly layers. Starting hundreds of yards offshore there were layers chasing other layers as they raced each other toward the shore until they all broke into white frothy foam as if in playful giggles on the part white, part grey sands. The noise of the breaking waves, the rhythm of the chasing dancing surf, the smell of the salty air duly spiced and flavored by the seaweed plus the nearby bushery combined into an enveloping sensory embrace that for Gemma embodied 'the beach'.

They trudged the remaining two hundred feet across the wide gently sloping beach down to the place where the wet darker sand fought with the dry grainy stuff and left their shoe and footprints in both as they washed their feet off. Gemma thought to herself, it's rather calm today. Normally there were vast scary cascades of crashing waves seeming to start quarter of a mile out, with the violently frothing surf literally booming nonstop. Looking up and down the wide expanse of sandy beach lined by coconut trees with dark green shorter mangrove plus windswept sea grapes, she felt tiny and vulnerable standing there taking it all in. The coconut fronds were only gently being tickled by the breeze making only slight chattering sounds compared to their typical violent flapping. Gemma was careful to avoid walking under those trees that were laden with dried coconuts. A small precaution to prevent brain damage and death from falling fruit she thought. This was not a normal beach where people went to have a fun bath. Too many had drowned there, she'd been told. The rip currents here were brutal and merciless. There were calmer, much safer, more fun beaches to go to, with protective reefs and bathtub like bathing areas, though they were a good bit further away from her village. The warm seawater lapped at their feet splashed over their toes and attempted to climb up their legs rudely trying to reach up to their knees. She could feel grains of sand, some fine and a few larger coarser grains ebbing and flowing between her toes and under the arch of her feet giving a quicksand type effect as the seawater ebbed and flowed. Standing there for a few minutes, Gemma said eventually, "Gosh fellas I enjoyed that hike, let's go by the bushery to see if we can see tittery." Those were tiny fishes caught by small nets in the bushery and made into delicious snacks resembling fishcakes. Gemma loved them!

They walked with anticipation back along the beach toward the bushery, finding that it had moved considerably from where it had been before. In the battle between sea and river's end, the sea was implacable and the bushery found it necessary to be flexible. It went wherever the sea and shifting sands allowed it. This wide confluence of river meeting the sea, was like a restless animal, always moving morphing like a soul in purgatory. The violent scratching sounds of crabs ducking back into to their holes increased with their approach. There it was lying languidly, dark brown with a slight green tinge maybe, visible as they came up a slight rise stepping carefully among the crab holes. They had had to approach under the shade of mangrove, poisonous manchineel and sea grapes. They all knew better than to even touch those terribly poisonous manchineel plants, as the accidental wipe of contaminated fingers after so doing in the eye, could lead to blindness. She marveled at how the mangrove trees with their intensely dark leaves managed to hold themselves up on their stilts out of the water and how they were strong enough to resist the winds, waves and strong tides. Although the water was dark colored here in the shade, at the very edges where it was shallow, they could make out small darting fishes and even small crabs scuttling back and forth, disappearing into the deeper opaquer water. They stared at the spectacle for a few minutes quietly and then made their way slowly over to the very edge of the bushery where the river flowed over dirty looking wavy scalloped sand to merge with the seawater.

There were fewer coconut trees here, and it was all bright sunshine. Thus, they could take their time walking slowly along and observing the wild life more openly with sea birds squawking warnings loudly as they approached. There were several different kinds and sizes of birds. Some were regular seagulls, but there were also terns and a few ducks on the freshwater side. A lonesome grayish white crane stood seemingly motionless in the shallows, waiting to spear a fish with its sharp long beak. Large seabirds lazily circled overhead never seeming to flaps their wings. People said that there was an island close by where the elusive frigate birds kept their nests. Gemma wondered whether some of those larger ones way up high in the brilliant blue sky amidst the cotton ball puffs of white clouds that she was looking at might be the super long distance gliding frigate birds.

She decided that she would bottle it all to take it home with her if that were possible. It was just so beautiful here. Alex had a stick and was playfully pushing it in the water to herd the little crabs and some of the wading birds actually came closer as if to take advantage of the help to grab at those crabs. Otherwise they kept quite still, taking in the whole scene. Gemma was breathing in the view, the scents, the sounds, the atmosphere. She really loved being at the beach, and although it really wasn't much beyond a mile way, regretfully only occasionally and sporadically did she get to come here. This wasn't a good beach on which to bathe and swim. Many who had dared to swim here had met their end with the unpredictable riptides. Mom had said that the meeting of the river and seawater helped to create bad conditions here. One thing that Gemma noticed was that the few fat pork trees sitting amongst the sea grapes that she observed did not have fruit. It made her sad to not be able to savor the greenish slightly pink tinged loose skinned puckered fruit, which on biting yielded a thin marshmallow textured white flesh that was 'oh so good' to suck on. Then would come the relish for Gemma who liked the unusual, biting into that seed. The flesh therein was hard, nutty, but with a somewhat bitter after flavor. She didn't care that others simply threw the nut away. Bitter things were appealing to her. They spent about an hour running around on the beach, on both sides of the bushery before embarking on the trip home. They did not go to the extreme end of the bay where one could climb over the jagged dangerous rocks of the headland to visit some pools where colonies of cylindrical sea cucumbers known locally as sea cucus, that much misunderstood creature, were known to congregate alternately pulsing and sucking in the water as they innocently filtered for their food.

This time they used the normal road including the dilapidated bridge to cross the same river that they had followed to get down there. As the three of them headed back to her home in Zion, Gemma enjoyed looking at the short weeds on the side of the road as they passed patches with intensely blue and purple flowers. It was so unusual to see blue live things in nature she thought. Once in a while she had spied some climbing vines with large blue tulip like flowers that someone had named wild potato vine. When she had spied another vine, also with blue flowers, a helpful knowledgeable grandma from her village had told her with a grin that it was called blue pea pussy vine. Going closer for a good look, Gemma thought that it only cursorily looked a 'little rude' but was otherwise really a cute brilliant blue flower with a truly unique form. That woman just had a 'dirty mind' she concluded.

One of Gemma's favorite things to do was to run alongside the public roadways, like to and from the shop, when her mom sent her to buy some flour and sugar and to do so as fast as possible to see the plants on the banks moving blurringly fast in the opposite direction. She fancied that she was going almost as fast as the bus. So, she challenged Alex and Randall to a brief dash between two houses a few hundred yards apart. She had lost to the much faster boys, but they ended up having to run in earnest when some dogs took it as a challenge to chase after them as they ran.

When they passed by the second rum shop in the first junction, she heard some of the young men under the 'lean to' slapping dominos and she recognized a couple of them to be the ones who routinely harassed her and every young lady who passed by with comments and whistles. "You're coming to come little skinny thing. When you go put on some weight and grow some taetae girl? You front bone look good you know; you go make good children one day!" Thankfully, those walking perversions were all caught up in their games. She did not relish having nasty things said to or about her at any time, but especially not when she was with her compatriots. It was one of the reasons that she dreaded having to go to the shop and walking past this area of her village. She rejoiced that mom G had some juice to quench their thirst when they got back home, surely, she would have noticed that they looked hot and tired which is exactly how they felt. Visits to the beach were a famous way to get dry in the throat. Mom G asked, "Did you all have fun with your little trip? I hope you all didn't go play on those people's water wheel. They are very cross about that you know." They all kept 'Mum', not a squeak! Better to say nothing and make no admissions, than to have to tell a lie was the prevailing sentiment. After profuse thanks, Alex and Randall left with instructions to, "give you parents my regards ok" from mom G.

Cereal as usual was overjoyed to see Gemma and she had patted his head, rubbed his forehead and sleek jowls, prompting him to lay down on the rickety front steps next to Gemma's sister Mavis, who had been lounging there already, combing her hair. Her sister was getting ready to leave her clerical job at the banana boxing plant to take up teaching at one of the nearby Primary schools and lately she seemed to have a thing about one particular young man. With that, she had shown more interest in her appearance and her hair. Cereal was thoroughly enjoying his back and belly rub, eyes closed. When he sensed Gemma slacking in her duties, he would moan a little. Gemma would recommence giving him the attention he felt he deserved and his eyeballs would roll back in his head, one of his back legs kicking reflexively in pleasure as she rubbed and scratched him here and there. That dog really was sure that he was human and Gemma was his personal groomer based on the way he behaved.

Gemma in the meantime, had gone into a bit of a reverie, harkening back to the time two years ago when she was returning back from a trip to the beach, just like the one they'd just come from. They'd seen Mr. Busby who tended a shop along that road, standing over a dog that was nursing some cute puppies under the side of his shop and he was looking somewhat concerned. Being the inquisitive little kids that they were, they had paused to take in the scene, then walked closer. Mr. Busby in answer to their enquiries had explained that his dog of Alsatian breed had had babies for a neighbor's mutt dog and was now rejecting the smallest pup, pushing it away and not feeding it. He was concerned that the pup was not going to make it. Gemma had piped up, "Can I have it to nurse it back to health?" To which Mr. Busby replied, "Are you sure. It is a lot of work you know. You will have to feed it every two hours and keep it inside the house and warm." Gemma who had been expecting a "no", since he obviously sold his pups, perked up with hope and said, "I will take very good care of him." Mr. Busby had said, "Ok you can have him, you seem to be a good kid, let me give you some milk to hand feed him."

Gemma then could hardly believe her good fortune, and the thought hadn't even occurred to her that she should ask her mom G first. So gently picking up the tiny warm helpless clump of puppy, she opened her little jersey and laid it against her chest with her hand underneath to keep it in place so it wouldn't slip down to her belly and with the other hand holding the bag of milk, she said, "Thank you Mr. Busby" and went home. She couldn't even remember passing by Eslyn's home, one of her school friends. Mom G hadn't been cross about it, instead said, "It's a good breed." To Gemma's surprise, mom G even was heard to say the word 'cute' in reference to the poor little thing whose eyes were still tightly shut. The little pup lived on Gemma's chest, sleeping with her inside the house and she devised a way of dripping a few drops of milk down her finger into the pup's mouth and it learned to gently suck on her little finger. Gradually it grew stronger and Gemma doted on it, even running home from school on breaks to make sure to feed it. She named the pup Cereal after his pale creamy color, and now it was reaching up to her mid-thigh and they did everything together. Cereal followed her everywhere even to the outdoor toilet and shower and eventually to the shops to make groceries as well as to school. He was a robust two-year-old and he quite clearly believed himself to be a human. Recently Gemma had taken a couple of photos of him and of them using the old film camera that her brother now in the USA, had left for her. Maybe once a year at most, she could send up one roll of film for him to process and post back to her. It was beyond expensive to just buy the roll of film, much less to try to have it processed in the island of Camerhogne. It had been wonderful to see the results of her snaps from two years ago- her first set ever. This was true delayed gratification for poor folks.

As she gently caressed Cereal keeping a sharp lookout for that pestilence of dogs, fleas, she marveled at how clean his skin was in the transient furrows created by her fingers parting his very short fur. His cool dark nose wiggled side to side when her fingers swiped momentarily over it, maybe with a hint of irritation. Even in his now sleepy state, eyes closed, it was interesting to her how his ears perked up with sounds of happenings out by the road such as the neighbor throwing a bucket of dirty water out her back window. His nose also periodically wiggled open and closed as if sampling the scents flowing by his nostrils and his whiskers along his snout twitched nervously along with those movements. She had noticed him doing that too even when sleeping in her presence, maybe while dreaming she surmised. He seemed very comfortable taking daytime naps when she was with him and he felt he could relax while she was alert. Just then, she happened to look up and through the partly opened door, there sitting on the side table was a tray with some fruits including condicion, cherries and golden apples.

Gemma's eyes must have opened wide in surprise and her older sister just happened to notice. She said "Didn't your friends tell you that they'd brought a bag of fruit for us?" Gemma shook her head 'no'. "Yes, Randall brought it from his mother and even Alex came with some golden apples. They must have put it on the steps while you were downstairs below the house to tie up Cereal so he wouldn't tag along with you on your hike. We've already sampled it, Mom and I, so go get yourself some."

Gemma promptly gave up on giving Cereal his most loved massage and he sprang awake as soon as she stopped, as he sensed her in change of mood. There was a sudden spurt of saliva in Gemma's mouth and a strange little twinge below her tongue. She could almost taste the twinge of sharp tartness that was about to come when she would bite into the puckering crisp yet soft flesh of the condicion fruit that looked almost like a little preserved cucumber thingy that mom G had her taste once called 'pickles'. As she got up to go wash her hands in the outdoor pipe where a sliver of common blue soap lived permanently alongside a loofah for scrubbing purposes, she spied a few damsons too on the fruit tray. "Oh my gosh, I can't wait," she thought as her mouth made more juice! Cereal was up with her walking alongside as if saying while looking up at her inquiringly, "What's wrong, what's the hurry all of a sudden my human?" He watched her impatiently as she washed her hands and headed back to the front steps, his cold moist nose literally bumping the back of her thigh. When she got inside and she went for a damsel first, popping it into her mouth; his tail fell from the up and alert position into a dejected droop and he plopped himself down on the floor with a now bored expression as if to say, "You Gemma, you humans, always eating such nasty foods, fruits aagghh." Yet he kept an eye open looking at her working that damson inside her mouth, paring off the juicy but acidic flesh between her tongue and teeth before popping the seed six inches from her mouth into her waiting hand. With a backwards fling of her hand, the seed flew through the window which was wide open as the window blinds were tied to the sides.

Gemma by now was seated on one of the rickety chairs across from mom G's sewing machine and excitedly chomping into the turgid flesh of that nice green condicion. When she bit into it, droplets of moisture exploded into her mouth and a few escaped onto her jersey too. Bursting with flavor and sharp tanginess was how she liked it and that was how it was. Her sister looked at her through the open door and shook her head, "You're not right, you know that. You're the only person in this house who loves that sour stuff like that. I tasted it and had to throw most of it away." Gemma was aghast at the thought of such delicious fare being thrown away half eaten, but didn't say anything. Just like her sister to bite into something that she knew already that she wouldn't like and then discard it she thought. "What a waste, why did she even try to eat it, did she expect it to not be acidic?" she thought. She didn't say anything out loud though, just kept on munching. She wouldn't need dinner today. Cereal was thoroughly bored and was sprawled full length sort of asleep by then.

Now fully hydrated from her battle with all that juicy fruit, Gemma rejoined her sister on the step sitting there contentedly swinging her legs, looking at their yard. Up the hill she took in the escarpment where the mongoose families lived. Down a bit from there, were her and mom G's pigeon pea trees coated with ants. They had to do battle with those ants to harvest the peas over the Christmas holidays not long ago. They always won in the end, but not without lots of 'bumps' to show from ant bites. Hopefully they might get a second crop from them, she thought. There were quite a few yams with extensive vines up there along the bank, but they had to run the gauntlet with the mongoose tribes risking life and limb to dig them up occasionally. One person had to stand guard with a long stick while the other did the digging. Who wanted to die of rabies? That was a real risk on the island of Camerhogne.

Her mind went back to the time a few years ago when they'd had a pig, because it was in the upper garden area that it was often tied out to graze. Nothing useful could be planted then in that area. At night it was brought to its little pig pen to evade the known and unknown village thieves. Of course, the pig was so cross, that short of drugging it with chemicals to force compliance, it would be hard to coax it away without lots of noise and maybe injury to the thief. That pig was a true wrecking ball of an animal. Oftentimes it was necessary to tie it over by the driveway or down in the bush close to the river, taking great care that it didn't damage people or their crops. The brute was quite literally taller than Gemma at that time and she had seen it have its way with her mom and brother too. One toss of its head at her poor Dad whom it hated, would see him flung a few feet away; she had seen that with her own eyes. The piggy was much kinder to Mom G who had been his nurturer from since piglet stage of course. When it was handheld by chain, to move from one spot to another or to allow it to graze, if there happened to be a patch of juicy grass that it took a liking to, woe be unto the fool who got the idea that they could pull it away. They had had to get it butchered shortly thereafter and good riddance, Gemma and really just about everyone had thought. Unfortunately, they did not have refrigeration and had to sell all the meat but for a few meager pounds. She did get to taste a bit of blood pudding though, made from its blood and its tripe that had been washed out in the river, its blood, farine made from ground up dried bitter appropriately processed manioc (cassava root), salt and pepper. Only then were they able to reclaim that hillside for vegetable cultivation.

On the edge of that upper bank area, where it adjoined the driveway, were some gorgeous flowering shrubs mostly crotons with their multicolored leaves sporting the kaleidoscopic browns, yellows, reds and purples of all shades plus three almost tree sized crepe myrtles bearing a mix of red, purple and white flowers. Bordering the driveway, there were also assorted shrubs, comprising cattails with their long pinkish red blooms, some roses and buttercups teeming with their colony of yellowish green fat caterpillars. That served to keep their yard bursting in color, in keeping with even grander color schemes up the hill at the Renwick's.

Some of her cucumbers with their yellow flowers and fruit at all stages of development that she'd planted, were even trying to climb up the pigeon pea trees. Those vines were hers. She took pleasure in inspecting them and following their growth daily. She'd planted them because she loved cucumbers the most. Her sister never ever wanted to do anything in the garden which was fine with Gemma. When her brother was here in country, he at least would help to clear the land with his cutlass and to till the soil with the fork. Apart from reading, no more correctly put 'devouring' books, this place - the garden, was where she could go to lose herself. Just watching the whole world of ants scurrying, bees flitting back and forth loading up on nectar and pollen, wasps of all types coming in for the ambush on other critters then flying away with their plump caterpillars bigger than them like old time blimps, was totally captivating. Her mom often had to call out to her, "Gemma what are you doing so long in the garden?" Her answer was most often, "Nothing Mom." At that she could expect to hear mom G to be mumbling loudly, "Nothing, nothing, you've been there how many hours now doing what, I don't know." At one stage of her development, Gemma was teased at school for being much lighter skinned than her compatriots and her response to being called 'Whitey bakae skin back tae tae,' was to parch herself in the sun. Being in the garden was one way that she strived to become as dark as possible.

There was an area off to the side of their garden where a stool of bananas lived. Some of the large dead leaves that were way taller than her, hung limply along their tall fleshy stems. As she had grown up, she had become attuned to the sight of those leaves transitioning from what they were, dried leaves, to ominous looking spirits as the evening light faded and night inexorably won the battle. Sometimes those dried hanging leaves looked even more scary under a full moon. In fact, peeping through the blinds and even cracks in the wall, Gemma would follow the changing appearance of those leaves as they waved in the breeze. Following its changing appearance over time helped her to become less scared of the dark. There was still the odd occasion that she somehow was caught returning from the shop late at dusk. Now, when she got to the midway point between the shops in one junction and where her home was situated at the other junction of roads, at that very dark foreboding area under that great big tree where everyone said the soucouyant, the lajabless and the Mama Maladee most assuredly lived, she found it to be a bit less threatening to her. She gradually began to relate the previously ominous sounds there to normal scraping of branches one on the other as that happened in the daytime too. The rising ruffle of the wind exciting the fronds of the nearby coconut trees as they chirped like schoolgirls happy to meet again and the rustle of the dried banana leaves too while looking like ladies in crumpled dresses walking toward her became less terrifying.

Of course, there were sometimes happenings that went unexplained but not always. Once she had heard definite footsteps that almost exactly mirrored hers in the bushes along the road. On a whim, with fear almost strangling her throat, she had called out, "Gleans, is that you?" Gleans who was young rastaman though older than her and quite eccentric, but who was well known to her, preferred to walk in the bush rather than out in the open street as normal people would. No answer came. So picking up a stone, she threatened loudly to start stoning down into the bush. That was when she heard, "It's me Gemma, don't stone me girl, I'm just going about my business." To that she said, "Ok Gleans, next time answer quicker, you scared me." Those were the happenstances that Gemma used to gradually begin the process of inuring herself against the old peoples' scare tactics.

With her brother gone, it was only Gemma and Mom G since her sister had no interest in gardening. Gemma could not handle the fork which was bigger and almost as heavy as her skinny little self. She would try though sticking its tines into the hard ground, standing on it, jumping on it and nothing would happen, nothing! Mom G would put one foot on it, rock it back and forth and its sharp tines would slowly work its way though protesting, into the hard ground. Then mom G would lean it, press down and backwards and another clump of earth would pop up making a ripping sound with earthworms, ants plus a myriad of nameless insects now exposed; all would go scurrying back into the now exposed soil. Then over and over again, mom G would do it while Gemma would be attempting to further break the clumps up with a cutlass and drop her cucumber seeds, corn or whatever other seeds in, before covering it up. Later on, Gemma would be back with a bucket of water into which she would dip a milk can with perforated holes and let the water fall right over each hole where she had previously planted those seeds. Both mom G and Gemma would take turns 'djouging' water to wet the plants when it was dry. After days of waiting and anxiously peering at the newly planted garden, there would be the gratifying appearance of whitish green shoots. Gemma would excitedly tell mom G, "They're growing Mommy, they're growing." She loved, with the exception of the creepy crawlies, everything about planting, down to the smell of the freshly turned earth!

Her eyes cast toward the lower part of their yard where mom G had a few pumpkin vines and they were bearing too. Not her favorite vegetable, she quickly and unhesitatingly thought. Something about the yellow thick soup that mom made with it to accompany the green figs as they called bananas or whatever else she could scrounge up for food, did not sit well with her stomach. Might it have something to do with her brother and even sister, telling her stories when she was much younger about its resemblance to a particular body function to deliberately turn her off it, so that they could scoop it out of her plate since they enjoyed it? It got to the point where poor Gemma would wash her little flour dumplings off with water after fishing them out of the pumpkin soup, while her much older siblings waited with anticipation for the now discarded soup. She remembered years ago, when mom G left the choice part of dinner for their father and he would come home stinking drunk and in no way interested in eating, how she and her siblings would compete for the spoils. With no refrigeration, it was 'use it up quickly' or it spoiled.

There were a few banana trees down there, an extremely delicious large bearing avocado, one breadfruit tree, a coconut short 'jelly' tree and a citrus gospo tree too. Further down the hill were her mom's prized tania and dasheen bushes with the latter being practically down in the approximately ten-foot-wide drainage ditch where water from several houses ran, plus natural drainage from the surrounding hills gathered when rains came. Being a hop, skip and a jump from the river less than a hundred yards away, it wasn't surprising to see crayfish, the reddish type that she believed to be more like the 'crawdads' she'd read about, and brown eels called yokas plus even criebos slithering around in the muck. The criebos were jet black, compared to the short stubbier dark brown of the eels or coelacanths types called yokas. The criebos really were small boa constrictors looking for rats and such. At least that's all she had caught them eating anyway.

Mom G always pointed out the silvery scum growing all over the dirty watery area and would tell her, "Don't go walking barefoot in there or playing there, 'cause you'll get a bad case of ringworm in your feet or hands!" Gemma didn't need any encouragement really. The stuff in there looked positively nasty and so she would try to go there only when it was somewhat dry and with some kind of foot protection. That meant donning mom's water boots within which her tiny feet floated as she valiantly tried to drag them along, when asked to go pick some callaloo which were the younger leaves of the dasheen plant. Sometimes those boots would become mired in the wet sticky mud and in attempting to remove the stuck boot, her foot would come flying out instead. So, she had learned a technique for such boot removal that involved holding onto the top of the offending boot with both hands and usually with an awful squelching sucking sound have it reluctantly pop out as she pulled with all her might. Also, it had happened several times to her that she had felt a sharp hard bump at the tip of the water boot as if being told 'go away'. Many times, she couldn't find the culprit, but when she did a couple of times, it turned out to be a yoka with its head barely peeping out of a cave like hole in the bank. It was an occasion for her to worry that had it been her toe on bare feet that she might have been bitten, and that added impetus to her resolve to never go into that dreadful swampy area without tall water boots on. If callaloo therefore was not available, she'd have to harvest the young leaves of the zeppina plant which grew with ebullience all over the yard with no encouragement. This 'Jamaican callaloo' wasn't as flavorsome as what Gemma considered the 'real callaloo', but it filled the hungry hole. They fried well with flour as a makeshift vegetarian 'fishcake', plus was used with ground provisions like yams, sweet potatoes, even with dumplings and fig, to 'stretch' the food as Mom G described it. Gemma who loved vegetables anyway, loved it in all its forms.

Flicking a fragment of that delicious golden apple from between her front teeth, she stared at the strange tree that was growing maybe five feet from the end of the steps. It was a mystery to her and everyone. Mrs. Maymay, which is what everyone called her, who lived along the same Potry road that she had just used to come back from the beach today, knew how much she loved to plant had said, "Come here little girl. I have this strange seed that someone gave to me and I don't know what kind of tree it will make. Plant it and let me know." It was big, furry and weirdly shaped like none she had ever seen, much less handled. She had turned it over and over in her hand peering at it and at home her mom G hadn't a clue. She'd brought it to some of her neighbors including Ms. Cici who normally knows everything, and even she did not know it's parentage, nor it's children. So, she had gone ahead and planted it anyway right where she could keep an eye on it, right in front of the step. Now it was about three feet tall with long spindly leaves and growing, but into what? No one knew for now what size or type of tree it would grow into.

Chapter 11.   Change is constant

So, carnival came and went, before Easter did the same. Then before too long primary school was out for her and her friends. The heavy rains came in June. There were several close calls with tropical storms headed their way, only to brush their island nation, but with heavy rains, flooding and lots of garden variety landslides. Sometimes for days the heavy drumming came on the galvanized roof, quite sleep inducing. Going to the shop meant walking in sheets of water, which was fun to play in generally but not when this continued day after day. Some of the neighborhood boys took pleasure in floating homemade boats in all of the ephemeral ponds. Most were made from coconut shells and even they grew tired, waterlogged and eventually sank. Those were umbrella-breaking rains particularly when the wind was also gusting erratically. Clothes, whether hung outside well under the house, or inside, stubbornly stayed damp. Dry firewood could not be found and all that had been stored under the house was used up. Getting charcoal was not an option as it meant crossing dangerously swollen creeks and rivers. Mom G would use her stores gingerly, mixing it with whatever half wet firewood that could be scrounged up. With wet firewood, there was lots of smokey fires leading to lots of tearing when it became necessary to coax the fire under the pot with fanning or blowing. So, it was back to the weak smokey kerosene stove which could barely handle more than a small pot. It was miserable. Sight of the sun, free and clear and shining bright was like a rebirth. Everyone celebrated by coming out of their houses to bathe in its warmth. People you hadn't seen in weeks walked the streets just to get out of their homes and have a respite from the mosquitoes and sandflies that had proliferated in the meantime. The drain at the bottom of the garden was roaring. The river was up to the bottom of the bridge and it was a spectacle to see. When it came over the closest and largest bridge to their home, only the largest trucks and buses would gingerly chance a crossing.

Gemma had found out that she was going to get to go to a High School Mt. Rush much closer to her home than the one attended by her older brother and sister at McDuff. Somehow lots had happened around that time that was surprising and even shocking. Although they'd grown up Catholic, Gemma's brother and sister had been coaxed somehow into attending the local Seventh Day Adventist church and had been doing so for years. In fact, that was where he had met his wife Wren. Although Mom G had stubbornly refused to honor dietary requests that they had made, including not cooking pork products and the like, somehow Ms. Cici had managed to lure Mom G to accompany her there for some special session. Mom G must have seen something that she liked. Both she and Ms. Cici started attending that church and Gemma got to go to the Secondary School affiliated with it therefore. It had all happened very fast, virtually overnight it seemed. All these 'new churches' had proliferated in this the northern part of the island nation, scooping parishioners away from the staid and unexciting Catholic and Anglican churches. So it was, that Gemma was now headed for an SDA secondary school about a mile and a half away uphill. At least bus fares weren't essential.

It was also a time of social upheaval with times being very hard for everyone. Even getting essential goods was by no means guaranteed. It was under this cloud of change and uncertainty that Gemma had to get Mom G to sew uniforms for the new High School, and to get books. This necessitated the big expensive trips to the capital city of Fredericktown to procure cloth and books. So, there was a new school and a topsy turvey political climate with a hard economic situation and a major church affiliate conversion for mom G. Gemma was transitioning from a relatively carefree though by no means sheltered childhood into an era of even more uncertainty as a newly minted eleven-year-old girl.

There was no alternative but to survive. A bag of books on her back, she excitedly survived her first day at high school, made new friends and grew apart from many of her old ones. By the end of her first year, confidence growing, she could barely remember the days of old. She and Randall still met and talked but he was going to a different secondary school and they didn't hang together nearly as much anymore. There were new teachers and teaching styles to adapt to, new upper-class students to learn about and their dirty tricks too, to ensure one did not get caught out by. Since she now had to go through new villages to get to and from school, there was a whole new world literally, to explore. It was exciting times for her, mixed with some fiendishly stressful moments.

Change suffused everything and in every aspect of her life. She got to sit in class with a wide variety of students, some like her who'd come from poor backgrounds, while others were from families who were obviously in better shape economically. Some came to school in their parent's motorcar and expressed great surprise to learn that Gemma had only one pair of regulation shoes, two pairs of uniform tops and only one skirt which needed to be washed and dried overnight if it got soiled! Gemma was careful not to take part when the discussions turned to 'drawers' as the older folks called girls underwear. She knew how she had to sometimes wash and wring dry those items which often were not fully dried by the next morning when it happened to be raining and the atmosphere was pregnant with dampness and humidity.

Going to the big high school provided her with the opportunity to further appreciate and interact with other characters whether it be fellow students, teachers or other villagers. Even meeting various families that were somehow related along the route to and from school provided lessons in petty snobbishness based on the 'oh you're from the poor uncle's side of the family yeah' attitude. One particularly obnoxious young man, a fellow student became an obsequious snot in class, always attempting to ingratiate himself with the science teacher who was a rather cute young lady. He couldn't seem to understand that his tactics were bereft of any subtlety and could only be perceived by even the most clueless in the class, as nauseating. There were also a couple of 'bragger' boastful boys in class and the worse part had to do with the fact that they mostly didn't need to be that way. Those two actually were naturally talented young men academically. Somewhere along the line, Gemma along with her friends thought that they were either born that way or had adapted to manipulating their circumstances using such totally transparent tactics.

Pretty soon, her new routine stabilized, which involved getting up earlier than she used to have to do for primary school. She awoke at about the same time really as before, but now had to 'hurry up' out of her bed more promptly as mom G perpetually called it. No more lallygagging was the other term used by mom G. "Don't you remember how fast your older brother and sister had to prepare?" Gemma was asked. "No I do not. I was too young then," Gemma said to herself silently. To give her Mom G such an answer would be looked upon as the height of petulance and might indeed draw not just a tongue lashing but likely too a 'rap' delivered to the top of her head by mom G's hand. Gemma knew to never underestimate the striking speed of mom G's hand. Snakes came to sit at her feet in order to learn how to speedily strike, Gemma smirked privately to herself. It was rare, but once experienced, never was a repeat rap sought after. School started at eight in the morning so she had to be hitting the road to tackle her first big Ponzfield hill, then some serpentine hairpin turns in the paved roads to be at school on time; that meant leaving by a quarter to seven. Of course, that meant that Gemma and her buddies had to get creative on some mornings to straighten up their route and still have fun! They would create their own shortcut pathways to eliminate those long winding roads by running downhill then back uphill from the start of one corner to the next. That meant scooting through various the farmers' nutmeg, cinnamon, breadfruit tree and cocoa cultivation. Such short cuts could only be attempted anyway when it was stone dry. So, she would privately admit, maybe they didn't shave much time off the journey, but fun they had trying. Also, every now and again, there would be some extra bonus; ripe fruits might make themselves available.

She and her fellow students made the best of those five years as they traversed the time span from Form one to Form five. There were challenges at every stage though, including situations involving the lack of teaching staff which meant that they had to join forces to read, discuss and literally teach themselves after procuring the syllabus. Sometimes they were able to borrow notes from other students like her old friend Randall, attending other secondary schools who had qualified teachers in a particular subject area. Looking back, she'd been able to accept that it wasn't all bad. It engendered self-reliance, resourcefulness and hard work.

There was the 'munerva' the old walled shell of a sugar mill long missing its windmill dating back hundreds of years, overgrown with large vines bigger around that Gemma's waist. Gemma and lots of fellow students found ways during their break periods, to shimmy up and down those vines despite the risk of collapse of the old structure upon them. This would be followed up by adventures galore on the homeward trip from school. Again, every fruit tree in season would be on the radar of Gemma's group. Sometimes it involved ingratiating themselves with the land owner with the proper greetings and even helpful acts to be rewarded with 'help yourselves to some mangoes children'; those were the magic words. Trees hanging over the road with ripe fruits when not being directly observed by the owner was prime target for 'stoning'. Some of the youngsters were quite accurate and able to hit the ripe fruit even when it was coddled among multiple still green ones. Of course, this was yet another opportunity for competition, fun and wagering.

Gemma had also gotten involved in Pathfinders club for boys and girls. There was marching and playing, camping and hiking. Of the most interest to Gemma was the hiking to the nearby mountains of Coublal as well as bush navigation trips to nearby beaches. It was thoroughly enjoyable and offered the one major outlet for her beyond the drudgery of her existence. It was a reflection of her growth that she did not see a trip down into her neighborhood woods of Kanhook as the 'exotic adventure' anymore. Now discovering gems involved travel much further afield into the capital city to the National Museum, the botanical gardens with its glorious flamboyant trees displaying their red flowers, the most popular mile long white sand beaches, as well as a few black sand ones, plus other historic locations and sites. She had grown up enough to no longer be scared of some of the cultural things like going to light candles on the graves while eating asham made of ground up parched corn mixed with brown sugar during the 'all saints' night. She marveled as she realized that there was the occasional house located within the cemetery with people actually therein. How scary she thought it would be, to have to face almost daily burials in your own yard. Although she wondered whether it would maybe be entertaining to watch the shenanigans associated with those burials. People jumping into the open graves, fainting, screaming, shouting all kinds of weird stuff to and at the dead body might, though sad, be a bit humorous too. During all this period of her life, of growth, increased self-discovery and personal development, she also continued her voracious reading, gobbling up novels of all sorts plus slightly enlarging her repertoire of friends.

Among the new friends she had developed was a young lady called Susie who was a friend of her friend Arlene. Together Gemma, Arlene and Susie somehow increasingly began to spend time with each other. Susie lived a good three miles and several villages away and came from a large family of six youngsters. They did share the same religion now and for some reason they just 'clicked'. Passing time for them meant the odd trips to the nearby beach, looking at the occasional film shown by entrepreneurs at the village school hall and just meeting to 'chit chat'. Otherwise, Gemma spent her time engrossed in her little garden, reading or out working part time whenever the opportunity presented itself. This was particularly so when school was 'out' and she was on vacation.

She had gotten to spend some quality time with her Godmother Mrs. Renwick before she'd passed, when Gemma was close to the end of her High School sojourn. She'd taken pleasure in meeting the grand children of Mrs. Renwick when they had come visiting. They were all older than her and the oldest, Christian seemed determined to introduce Gemma to new culinary experiences. That included Gemma's first experiences with sushi, lobsters which they could afford but her family couldn't, shrimp, caviar, fancy chocolates from America, spreadable pate', fancy cheeses, strange looking mushrooms and even cuts of meat done 'rare'. Some she relished, having read about them over and over again; others she regarded with utmost suspicion. Bloody oozing meat that Christian described as having been passed between a 'candle and a lightbulb' invoked the utmost disgust. Just watching him eat it, seemed a death-defying experience to her. 'Definitely not interested' was her response to him repeatedly offering her a bit of it. Other offerings like the 'fish eggs', as she chose to think of the caviar, was taste sampled but not loved.

She'd much rather shimmy up the many guavas, mango trees, plum trees that Mr. Renwick had planted all over his yard and in his fields than partake in some of Christian's exotic stuff. Funny how she adored grinding her teeth on an almost green guava, while leaving the fully ripe ones for the other humans and the birds. When she did go on those fruit tree jaunts however, the one major note to self was to make sure that the bull was not in close proximity to any of the trees near her. The savage animal had caught her once. It had then proceeded to corral her there by staying under her tree and then the evil one did his best to evict her by butting the tree with his head and bumping it with his body while watching her crossly and snorting viciously. She remembered being stuck there for what seemed like hours, while desperately wanting to empty her bladder and not being able to. She was eventually rescued by one of Mr. Renwick's workers who happened to be deaf mute but very friendly to her, since she had painstakingly taught him to count money so that people he worked for couldn't take further advantage of him and his disability. She figured that the bull was objecting to her trespassing on his territory. Yes, she was not on friendly terms with Mr. Renwick's cattle. Overall though, Christian had meant well and she did have fun when he was around. It seemed that he enjoyed exposing the little neighborhood girl to those unusual treats. For her it was an excellent opportunity to broaden her horizons.

Gemma took to babysitting initially as a favor to a family friend, then to earn a little money that would come in handy for everything from shoes to books. Eventually she got to helping Mr. Ocallahan in his local shop at busy times, serving village customers who came to 'make their groceries'. Mom G at one point, before Gemma's dad had passed used to keep a small shop, so the whole thing wasn't too unfamiliar anyway to Gemma. Then she got a little job in the regional town of Granvillevale selling with a little wizened lady of Indian extraction called Mrs. Allie. That was when Gemma was in Form Four, and just after Mom G had emigrated to the USA to join her son. Gemma's sister had gotten married to her beau and had renovated certain parts of the old wooden falling down house that had been their home all along. Gemma was able to buy her very own mattress and proudly pay to have it tied down on the public bus to bring it to the home. Gemma had been able to contribute in small ways through her earnings. She often had the chores of taking care of her sister's baby especially the first one to be born, all night long since she was the most sensitive to the baby's cries it seemed. It was stressful because it was at a time of intense study for exams with poor to no teachers at all for instruction, while preparing for the all-important GCE Exams.

Along her route to her Secondary school were several farms. There was one in particular that was run by young people and concentrated on growing vegetable cash crops that at times needed a burst of labor. She had taken to volunteering her labor whenever she could spare some time to do so, mostly on weekends but even during the week when school was not in session. So, Gemma could be found 'tek and tek' with the other young people planting, weeding, watering and eventually harvesting their fields which was spread over several acres on a hillside. Gemma would get to proudly carry bags of produce home to her wonderful mom G. Aside from the fact that she truly enjoyed engaging with the land and exercising her 'green thumbs', it in no small measure contributed to her little family's food security. She also enjoyed the genuine respect, appreciation and even friendships from those folks who were often older than her and did not have as much prospects to make progress educationally. For them, it was likely a very positive self-affirming experience to have a sharp pretty young lady by any standards, in Secondary school, come and enjoy mingling with them to do what many others would consider 'dirty work'. Gemma always insisted on keeping her head screwed on just right! She knew where she wanted to go, more or less, and was prepared to do the work to get there. She smiled to herself when she took the time to think seriously about such things, "I know where I definitely don't want to end up."

Chapter 12.   Gone to the capital

The next year, she was out, done with High School having passed her GCE Exams and at the urging of her principal entered the Nurse and Midwife Training Program in Fredericktown. There she would stay in the provided nurses's housing at the compound of the General Hospital. She even acquired a boyfriend who lived in her same village of Zion and with whose parents, especially the father, she'd had a warm relationship. That man had been somewhat of a drinking buddy of her dad too, before he died.

Some say 'time flies when you're having fun', but during this period of nurse training, time seemed to drag though. It had been five long years of training. Her mom was gone, there was no really welcoming home to go to she felt, and she saw firsthand and up close the games people played by observing the behavior of the superiors under whom she trained, plus that of her fellow colleagues. Oh Lord, her main male mentor and godfather in life Dr. Benny passed. That had been gut wrenching to her. Poor Mrs. Renwick was long gone too. She winced at the memory of her trying to help sickly Mrs. Renwick years before push the boucan, the heavy moveable rolling roof cover over the large cocoa bean air dryer. A large looming shower was heading their way with dark heavy clouds and there was no one else around to close it. All of the drying cocoa beans would have spoiled if they'd gotten soaked. Mrs. Renwick had called her on the old windup telephone strung between their houses. So little Gemma had had to put her back against the rolling roof cover and she had pushed with all her might and they had savored the reward of it squeaking noisily as it had trundled slowly shut, saving lots of money. Even Cereal her true canine love also had passed, painfully poisoned somehow. The rumor-mill of the neighborhood seemed to conclude that the poor dog had drunk antifreeze. Who, why, would anyone want to do that to a harmless sweet dog? It was heartbreaking to Gemma. Seeing her dog from tiny pup to adult go down among all the other tragedies around her led to some resolve. It was then that she concluded to herself, "Life is so so short, live every day as if it's your last, girl."

Living down in the nurse's hostel had its drawbacks definitely. At least she was always just steps away from her workplace and didn't have to worry about paying exorbitant rents and unreliable bus transportation issues, so those were the positive aspects. However, it was boring and she had no ability to go work in her garden patch to reset her stress level. Then again it was very difficult to get sleep with fellow nurses going and coming at all times of the day and night, which they did for both work and play. They were a quite randy bunch too, with their male visitors who were not supposed to be there, jumping windows to get to them for courtly often noisy escapades. To make matters even worse, there were some terribly vicious creatures upstairs of her who were supposed to be her seniors and superiors whose version of 'hazing' the newbies involved pouring what smelt like 'stale pee' down between the floorboard cracks onto the initially naive ones below. So, it was like another village just with different players, some of whom were up to malign games that only they got pleasure out of.

After a while of enduring some of her colleagues' liberties with her drinks and meals and having on occasion been a witness to their wanton taking, Gemma had hatched a plot to perform a social lesson. Her resolve hardened after discussions with one or two of her closer friends there who had themselves been victims too. Returning after a hard day of work to realize that most of their drink was gone or there were finger-tracks all over their food in their plate with all the meat gone was a bitter pill to be faced with. Then oftentimes it would be too late to even find a restaurant still open. Furthermore, on their meagre salary, such a restaurant meal, even a simple roti meal would be exorbitant; restaurants catered mostly to tourists and the financially well-heeled.

Gemma was in the exact-her-revenge mode. She had come to realize that it was a few selfish colleagues who participated in that kind of behavior. It centered on a few 'lovely ladies' who were unhygienic and really not caring much for themselves, much less for others. She had overheard some of the suspects talking about partying, sharing each other's partners secretly and subsequently needing antibiotic treatments for their various conditions. No way, after such individuals sullied your meal, could you use the remnants therefore. There were indeed some interesting characters living in that nurse's hostel.

So, on one of her trips to her country village, she went to pay homage to the hitherto scary sand box tree at its residence in Zion, only a few hundred feet across from her sister's home. After carefully surveying the immediate area to ensure that no devils of either the human or supernatural kind were lurking, she went about rummaging amidst the roots for seeds. Those seeds with its powdery entrails were then processed by Gemma to make them suitable for mixing with foods and drinks. Having warned only her two close buddies, the wait began. Sure as night follows day, the scamps went at it, slurping up Gemma's deliciously presented drink. Then as sure as day follows night, the awful diarrhea that went on for days ensued. The situation stopped, at least for several months. It seemed that there was a dampened desire to eat other people's food, for a while, when you couldn't be sure whether it was safe to do so!

Gemma had had to get creative with her entertainment. One day, when she was walking along the carenage she met and befriended one of the fishermen who was offloading his small boat there. This was concrete walkway along the water's edge in the capital city Fredericktown's main port and after their long discussion he ended up inviting her to come with him on some of his fishing trips. He had about a twenty-foot small wooden boat with a little outboard engine and a pair of ores for back up. So, from then on when that elderly gentleman would be on his way out of the harbor to fish, he would keep a scan going for Gemma in case she appeared on the rocks and stones that she frequented down below her hostel. On the occasions that she was there he would pull in close by and have her hop in. Often times she sat on the rocks just enjoying the solace and quiet of the crabs scurrying around in the shallow water and the small often highly colorful fishes darting in and out between the stones while being very careful not to fall in because there were significant currents in that area. Like a lot of people from islands, she had never learned to swim. For her, it had become a favorite place to hang out and calm down. It was also quite fun to watch the large and small vessels enter and egress from the harbor that was so well protected by two jutting opposing headlands. Some of them were quite large tourist ships with thousands of passengers, some of whom would even wave to her.

Even though the practice was discouraged by the authorities, often times there were young men swimming around the parked tourist ships who would dive in to retrieve and of course keep the coins thrown in by said tourists. Over the years she ended up having multiple trips that were quite fun with her elderly fisherman friend. So, he would then calmly launch out a half a mile or so out and set his nets and occasionally do so some rod fishing too. Gemma would sit in the boat as it rocked back and forth and help by bailing the water out of the bottom of the boat as it slowly seeped in. She would enjoy just gazing back at the land and its beautiful topography with its homes some gingerbread style, others palatial and even others shack like. She loved how those structures stacked up the hillsides terrace style decorating the rising terrain, like colorful icing on the tiers of a giant wedding cake. The hospital sat up on top of its own cliff like hill and the nearby majestic old fort that was built since the seventeen hundreds towered over it. The many quaint commercial buildings set against the background topography draped in mostly green vegetation interspersed with flashes of yellow and red flowering trees were part of the picture that she stamped into her memory banks.

The tiny little buses and cars scurrying along the carenage and other roads up and down the hillsides reminded her of the busy ants around their mounds. Sometimes the two chatted about his family or hers or even the happening news, but a lot of the time, they each were able to quietly ruminate on their own thoughts. Gemma looked forward to their little trips and the gentleman clearly enjoyed it too. Also, when she was with him, he did not have to worry about the periodic manual bailing-out of the seawater that constantly seeped in!

For complex reasons Gemma had gotten to a point of feeling that Zion was not home anymore, but she still did her best to visit her sister's home occasionally. Being with her little nieces and nephew made it worthwhile and they sure seemed to enjoy the little sweet and savory gifts she brought. When the day came for her to leave for the US, even though she had completed her training to be a certified Nurse and Midwife, there was no hesitation. Her boyfriend had not been able to shake the village traditions that she'd witnessed while growing up, flitting here and there with various flings and little mouths in cribs. Also, she had seen enough of the politics of the day plus the pettiness even within the nursing hierarchy too, that a clean start made sense and she felt ready for a change. Her big sister did not have much of an interest in emigrating, as she was content with the life she had built for herself in Camerhogne. Gemma though vowed that she was going 'even if she had to harelip the governor!' She knew it wasn't going to be a bed of roses, but she just didn't see any old nurses on the island nation of Camerhogne whose lifestyle she wanted to stay to emulate either.

Looking around her, she had taken stock of her little trio comprised of Arlene, Susie and herself that had coalesced around the end of her secondary school experience. Susie had recently, along with her sibs emigrated to the US to link up with their parents who'd been toiling away to create good conditions for them up there. Arlene had snuck away to go to Medical School. During her time in nursing school, one of her pastimes had been to visit with Susie who had become a teacher in a primary school and the de facto parent of all her younger siblings. Thus, when they'd finally gotten the call and made the trip up to the US, Susie had made it known that she was going to be eagerly awaiting Gemma's arrival. Gemma's own father's undeclared daughter who was around the same age as Mavis had moved too, just like her dad's much older acknowledged outside son and daughter had done, all gone to the great USA. All of those impulses were pushing her to take her mom's request to come meet her very seriously. She had also been noticing the same unpleasant tendencies in her boyfriend to adopt the typical man of Zion behavior which was a 'turnoff'. "Why throw diamonds at the feet of pigs," she had heard tell. "You lose the diamonds and if the pig even notices it at all, with no taste nor flavor to it, it just tramples it among its droppings, that's all." Gemma had vowed to not develop her life in the same pattern that was ubiquitous all around her with this wild sown seed, and dispersed family spread out among multiple women. In her head she said, "No way Jose, not happening to me!"

Her sojourn in the capital of Fredericktown had been interesting. It was like an expanded Zion village with much the same dynamics. There was the political ruling class who always seem to be in government and the diplomatic corp, who like chameleons and lizard like wood slaves, changed their colors and flavors so that they thrived no matter which official party won the elections. Their monied backers, the real power-brokers, owned the few remaining large tracks of land, old estates that often were no longer productive. Mostly too they also owned the large wholesale and retail houses, inter island ferries and were major shareholders in larger corporations like the bottling plants that often were spread over several island nations. There were the professional classes, the lawyers, doctors, bankers, architects and their ilk. The middle class included the higher ranking government workers, small business owners, established nurses, teachers and even some of the more well-to-do farmers. The menial workers, small-plot farmers and a whole host of others including the officially unemployed made up the large base of this pyramid. It was fun for Gemma to compare the different elements of her society with that of her village Zion. There were multiple opportunities to observe and interact with these various strata since they were her patients. She remembered one of those men asking her to make him a cup of coffee, a chore she had never had to contend with ever before. Of course she quickly learned how, but it was illustrative of their differences in upbringing and lifestyle. Not even at the Renwick's who were considered country rich with an extra beachfront house too, had she been exposed to brewing coffee. Plus she was able, even if she did not think of it being necessarily fortunate as much as educational, to encounter many others of different societal strata in the course of her sojourn in the capital. She was indeed grateful for her tremendous exposure to the variety of real folks plus those from her literary fictional encounters; long live books and reading! She had to conclude that people were the same all over.

The one thing that she vowed as she was leaving was to check up on that young man now a full doctor, studying in the US who she had met on the beach in La Anse, while they were both students.

As she remembered it, he had been sitting at the base of a sea grape tree, feet in the sand with what seemed to be a textbook studying. She and her nurse friend had come to the beach that morning after the short walk from the bus stop, noticing that he had looked up at them with a warm welcoming smile before putting his head back down in his book. However, after a while, Gemma had begun to disrobe and they'd realized that he had leaned back on the tree trunk and was unabashedly staring at her. Of course, her friend had then egged her on to 'give him a show'. Well, the young man had gotten up and with a broad smile came over to introduce himself as Martin, a medical student. He then explained that he had seen her on the hospital ward, but had not had an opportunity to introduce himself then. They had exchanged numbers and taken to occasionally calling. He often seemed to moonlight by working in the hospital laboratory to make extra money. So sometimes he would be able to call her from within the hospital itself, since he did not have the luxury of a home phone.

It had become obvious that Martin was hard working, resourceful and seemed quite motivated to advance himself. She herself had been extremely focused and driven in terms of protecting herself through the vagaries of life, as well as making academic progress determinedly. She felt him to be a kindred spirit in many ways. It was also obvious that he had come from poor stock, just like her. Although they'd never had an actual date, he had impressively gone out of his way to show his interest over the last four years of her training. She too was interested in seeing where their friendship might take them, but was wary of being 'used up' as she'd seen lots of nurses experience in the midst of their unbalanced relations with doctors. He had been steadfast in continuing to make contact by phone and letter throughout the years as they'd both progressed with their training. He was remarkable and intriguing to her in that there had been no one with whom she had ever been able to speak to for hours so effortlessly on a whole range of varied topics politics, religion, relationship, the future. Plus, he was friendly, quite 'bright' academically it appeared, down to earth. Importantly too, he was not bad to look at and had a great tickling baritone voice that one did not grow tired of. Even older nurses who happened to talk to him just on the telephone, would be on the verge of swooning at that voice. So, although life had gotten in the way to prevent them really getting together in person and exploring their compatibility further, she hoped that the opportunity would present itself when she got to the USA.

Her last months on the job was concentrated in the psychiatric unit with lots of night duty. Somehow, because of a mix-up between her physical appearance and that of a cousin of hers who was not even in the same stage of training, by a key superior, she seemed to have escaped having to travel to the remote outpost on a neighboring island. Instead, her cousin who looked very similar in appearance to her had been blessed with double duty over there, she had learned later. Gemma had not protested, quite simply because she had been unaware. Nevertheless, she had managed to avail herself with the help of some of her senior superiors, of the opportunity to deliver multitudes of babies and to get a good experience in her rotations in many of the other parishes' smaller hospitals.

In fact, it was during one such rotation that she'd made friends with a lady assigned there as an aide. She turned out to be an excellent cook and showed herself to be willing to help Gemma and her fellow training colleagues to learn to cook delicious wholesome meals quickly and efficiently. They generally had barely an hour to create a lunch in between the avalanche of sick villagers waiting to get their checkups, especially on days when the visiting parish doctor was in-house. There were often long lines of diabetics waiting on 'nurse to dress their sore foot'. By being her usual friendly cooperative self, she enticed the young lady to teach her how to make many dishes including homemade pizza and the 'throw everything-you've-got-in type of casseroles'. Gemma had never really gotten the opportunity to learn to cook before, while mom G had still been in the island. She had found herself always being elbowed out of the way like she was a 'royal nuisance'. Having eventually learned though from outsiders, she was even able to teach her sister Mavis how to make some of the tastier dishes she had come to master during her weekend visits to Zion.

Chapter 13.   To catch a plane

After all the stress of arranging time off, with her permanent resident visa in hand, Gemma walked the hill behind the hospital with its frangipani gorgeous scent, looking down towards the shapely harbor with parked cruise ships. The long white strip of sand LaAnse that she had frequented these last few years during her sojourn in the capital while in training, glistened in the distance. She would miss that. She would miss reclining on a towel totally relaxed just people-watching as kids played in the water, as bikini clad locals and tourists sauntered by. There amidst the hustle and bustle of water taxis in the harbor streaming white wakes down below her, the dark grey brooding shape of the coast guard vessel number one lay moored. Fond memories of a trip up the islands on that coast guard vessel facilitated by her knowing the skipper cracked her face in a smile. They had been classmates in High School and in those short few years he had catapulted himself up the ranks. That boat just absolutely sliced through the water, it was super-fast. She took in the view of the distant yellow poui trees on a headland in the waning sunshine of the evening sun. Standing amidst the flamboyant trees with their long colorful red flowers and brown seed pods, she said to herself, 'one day one day congotae, I am coming soon to mom G, coming to the USA'. She carefully picked her way back down the hill from the base of the ancient fort, avoiding loose gravels amidst the uneven pavement back towards the nurse's hostel making sure not to end up 'rolling down the hill pell mel'. It would be unfortunate at this late stage to get injured.

She would not miss the screaming, the erratic behavior of the ladies whose bodies were ready to deliver. By the sweat of thy brow, was truly real. There was very little available to help the birthing women other that a shot of demerol. As their bodies pulsed with pain, sweat pouring out, pushing, stretching, thinning, sometimes ripping, especially for the first timers she had witnessed the dramatic, strange things that sometimes happened. Many a time, she was forced to go flat on the floor with her starched blue uniform on, overlain with starched white ironed apron that they being trainee nurses, were forced to wear, to attempt to pull the screaming woman out from under the hospital bed. "I told him not to do it" was the most common refrain being shouted by the unfortunate young girls, now regressed into being the child they really were. In her head, Gemma could only say silently to herself, "Sorry young lady, but when you play with fire, guess what, you are going to get burned. Now it's time to give unto Caesar what belongs to Caesar. No going back now Darling." To the poor girl, she would say, "Be strong, the baby is coming dear, and I can't help you if you go hide under the bed, ok!" By the time she would get off shift, she would be stinking of amniotic fluid and other things that may have inadvertently come out from the 'nether parts'. Then she would have to hurry to wash and iron those infernally thick hard to manage clothes for the next day. At least she would sometimes be able to console herself with some mauby bark drink and some spicy sweet potato pudding back in the hostel.

Her last days in her island nation of Camerhogne were spent putting everything in order. Giving away what few worldly possessions she had to friends who wanted it, was a big part of it. She had been blessed to have been gifted many nice good quality sheets, bath towels and the like by her Godmother Mrs. Renwick when she had still been alive. They were still in good condition and between her sister and her friends she generously doled out those. Then she was climbing the steps to the airplane after passing through security, paying the exit tax and hearing the instructions 'flight so and so now boarding for JFK New York'. Gemma had once again looked at her boarding pass for the thousandth time, made sure her passport was in hand, shrugged on her carry-on and stepped forward with the throng. Soon she had felt the roaring of the engines, the little bump with their first movement as the pilot let off the brakes she guessed. The rest went by in a blur really. Then tired and cramped, she had joined the lines watching and reading carefully the overhead instructions and it was her turn to step up to the stern looking gentleman in the kiosk who peered searchingly out at her face from behind his glass enclosure. Finally, after many piercing questions her passport was stamped and she was 'admitted' into the United States of America.

Out into the crush and press of humans racing to get out from the confines of the airplane and customs, she launched herself. After grabbing her little suitcase off the carousel, she exited moving toward her brother waving amidst the waiting welcoming throng. It had been years since she had seen him and he had noticeably less hair on his head! He grabbed up her slender five-foot six frame in a tight brotherly hug and although she had known that mom G would be at work, she couldn't help but cast her eyes around looking for her. Her brother Damian said, "Mom G is not here. She is at work. You will see her on the weekend when she comes home."

Her brother dropped her off at his ex-wife Wren's apartment where she was to stay, along with their daughter and son. Relations between them seemed tense and sour as green grapes Gemma concluded. He headed out to Queens borough in New York City where he was with his new 'squeeze'. Gemma couldn't believe it; she was now in America. Everything moved so fast and all the streets looked the same to her eyes. There were long rows of similar looking buildings for blocks in every direction. She was now living with her sister-in-law, and her family; although mom G lived there and helped pay the rent, she was not there much, just on weekends. It rapidly became obvious that some big adjustments needed to be soon made in living arrangements. Thus shortly thereafter along with her mom and aunt, they moved into their own apartment. Gemma had tried her best to for a good relationship with her niece and nephew and to comfort them during this stressful divorce process. The kids were the ones who suffered the most during divorce. Her mom worked for a Haitian lady whose family seemed to be well to do. She Gemma quickly found a domestic job on the same street as Susie, her old buddy Susie, with whom she had linked up that same July of 1989 upon her arrival. Gemma was responsible as a nanny for a couple of kids from an orthodox Jewish family, while she studied for her Nursing Exams to get licensed to practice nursing in the USA.

Chapter 14.   Meeting the Martin

In September two months later, she was able to finally call that young man who was a physician in training just across from the borough of Manhattan New York, in Jersey City, New Jersey. Oh my, to hear his baritone voice again. He too was overjoyed to hear her voice on his answering machine and to know that she was less than an hour and a half away by train. He had quickly called her back when he got home and heard the message. That very next weekend he came walking down her street confidently with his little green now faded canvas bag that she still recognized from their beach encounter slung on his shoulder. Her world seemed to stop that afternoon, suspended as a few yellow-brown fallen leaves scratched erratically along the pavement from the slight breeze thrown up by the few passing cars. Across the street, some children played unabated on swings, others were bumping balls with attentive parents watching. He had on a faded looking pale green jeans type pants and a light bluish wind cheat jacket plus whitish sneakers as he confidently walked in his usual quick march style towards her. He had remained fit, trim and slender. When he smiled there was that cute little space between his upper two front teeth. It had been years since they'd seen each other, but it felt like yesterday. With his very slight almost pencil mustache, he looked good, unchanged from when she'd last set eyes on him in the flesh. My gosh she thought, "He looks good and he has the same little bag as on the beach when we first met!" They melted into each other's arms. Upon meeting mom G, hot from introductions, he declared that Gemma was to be his wife, Lordy. Mom G looked at Gemma with a momentarily questioning look, but hardly said more.

They met as often as they could and mostly made sure to speak with each other very often via telephone. She had been busy, preoccupied with her studies back home and had not been making a huge effort to try to maintain links with him as he had traveled to another island, thence the United Kingdom and from there to the USA for study and training. Now he was close to becoming an Internal Medicine specialist and was planning on also becoming a specialist in anesthesia, having graduated more than two years prior from Medical School. He informed her of his plans to build a home back in their Camerhogne island to accommodate his poor Grandma who had been in inadequate housing. He expressed the hope that it may possibly serve as a home for them too, as he hoped to return to give two years of service. The land had been purchased and the house construction had already started in Camerhogne on the basis of a loan. He, as a doctor but still a trainee, was still on a limited budget. He had purchased a small car and he promptly started giving Gemma lessons, telling her that she would need to be a competent driver and soon. There was the little inconvenient prior offer made to a girlfriend to have her visit and that had engendered some uncertainty to their budding relationship. Once that had passed and it had further clarified in his mind, what his choice needed to be, it was over. She too had been stumped by her former beau surprising her with a visit to New York with an offer of marriage. However, Gemma had mentally 'shaken the dust off her sandals' when she'd left Camerhogne and mentally was clear that returning to her vomit was not an option. Hurrah! They had both overcome challenges to their resolve and growing love for each other.

So, both Gemma and her now much more serious boyfriend Martin settled down to really build their relationship. The following July he had moved to Brooklyn New York to do his anesthesiology residency training and she helped to set up his apartment. In fact, she spent most of her time there with him. They tried to make up for all the years that they'd yearned for each other. Oftentimes they could be found enjoying the Liberty State Park in Jersey City soaking up each other and the atmosphere of the area. It was so wonderful looking across the Hudson River at the whole length of well-lit Manhattan and its World Trade Centers. Late in the evening and early night they would set up the tripod and take delayed exposure photos of themselves and the city or just the city. Gemma did lots of her driver training along the cobblestone macadam style roadways of that park. Other haunts included the views from the same World Trade Center buildings both day and night overlooking Manhattan and way out into New Jersey. Sometimes they mixed it up with similar, often late evening relaxing viewings from the Brooklyn Promenade, holding hands as they enjoyed the lights of Manhattan and the slow-moving tour boats oozing along, this time from across the East River. Atlantic City to simply get to feel sand again and the boardwalk was among their conquests. Trips further afield included one to Washington DC to afford her a little time with her older sister from a different mother, who had not grown up with them. Mom G had however sacrificed to find the tuition and other financial support to send her to High School.

Gemma's first snow was an absolute blast of an experience. Snow had been forecast and she had gone to bed early with intention to wake up in the middle of the night. That is exactly what she did. Rushing out from the apartment after seeing the white stuff floating down through the window accompanied by her little nephew, Gemma found herself outside on the stoop, no shoes on, dancing in the soft white fluffy stuff by the light of the porch as well as streetlights. Somehow with all that white highly reflective glistening sheet blanketing everything, it seemed so unusually bright. It was an incredible and magical moment to her. Years of reading about it, as well as the few times seeing it in the few movies she'd managed to look at, still had not prepared her for the actual beauty and the stillness that came with it in the middle of the night. She even opened her mouth to allow a few flakes to float on in, until her nephew pointed out that they were in the city of New York and as such those flakes may not be all that clean! It was only later that it dawned on her as to how dangerous it could be to have walked outside with no shoes on in the city where it wasn't rare to see the odd used hypodermic needle from drug users. They were not in a 'bad area' but nevertheless that could be a life threatening mistake. By the next morning though, the brownish black sloppy slippery mix that resulted, mauled by ploughing, cars, the feet of people and animals did not seem at all pleasant and certainly not pristine anymore.

The museums, the Bronx Zoo, exploring the nooks and crannies of some of the safer looking lower Manhattan districts, downtown Brooklyn, the Brooklyn Botanical Gardens which had been their wedding photo op venue, the Canarsie Park, all saw them frequently. In fact, all parks that looked interesting and appeared safe to them were fair game. They visited those sites in winter, spring, summer and fall. Getting out of their little apartment and exploring was their thing to do, with sometimes mom G receiving and accepting the invitation to have fun with them. Mom G was now very much enthralled with her tv and the soaps Gemma discovered, and was reluctant to even miss one episode, so she often declined their offers. Sometimes they drove but mostly the subway provided the best option since parking options were usually limited, difficult, expensive or all three. The once a year West Indian Carnival celebration was perused often and this sometimes provided the added opportunity to meet folks from back home who were either immigrants like them or visiting. Unfortunately, their financial situation still precluded any real immersion in the shows, whether Broadway or off Broadway. There was the dream to be one day able to do that though.

The Central Park concerts featuring World Class singers and bands were a huge hit with them especially when they were African or Caribbean. It was so unbelievably good to hear African singers of the caliber of Angelique kidjo in person, not to mention those top soca and calypso singers out promoting their music. Gemma and Martin could never seem to get enough of that. It was a true whirlwind of activity providing a great deal of fun and distraction from their job stresses. They were enmeshed within their own travel circuit soaking up new experiences the likes of which neither of them could even have dreamed of, while growing up poor in their respective villages.

The simpler things in life often taken for granted just on their street lined with brownstone houses were an eyeful to them. The light green verdant growth of the shade trees growing out of squares of exposed soil amidst the pavement in spring, slowly graduating to mature green in full summer and thence to brown flecked yellow with scaling multicolored bark in fall did not go unnoticed. Every season brought new discoveries, new vistas and new experiences to her. The first snows very early in the morning with glistening glints or sometimes fluffy lightness was absorbed visually, before the throngs of people, cars, birds and dogs all came out and churned it into a dirty looking dark blackened mess. Yet even then, often far later into the day or days, the walls and parapets would assume thick afro-like caps of white snow and ice. In time, icicles like stalactites up to foot in length appeared hanging threateningly from every gutter, roof edge and other elevated structure. On occasion after a particularly heavy period of snowfall, one would be rewarded with utter quiet early in the morning as hardly anyone stirred. That was such a rare though brief moment of peace in the city that never sleeps. After particularly large snows, the cars lining the streets looked like large pebbles in a stream, indistinct bulges that stood out only slightly from where one remembered the sidewalk and main thoroughfare to be.

The air would be still then, but for maybe the distant rip of a passing jet or a siren; there was always some siren blaring in the city. Then slowly there would be the harsh grating scrape of someone attempting to shovel out the entrance to their front door or to unblock the basement door to their underground lair. The tires, engines, the grating noises of large tractors and ploughs would soon begin to intrude though. Even in little backyards and small neighborhood parks, before even the children ventured forth, spidery tracks from birds and squirrels, later dogs and cats would mar the clouds laying on the earth as the soft fluffy snow seemed to them. It was with amazement that Gemma welcomed these vistas. Martin who often had to be up early to trek the half a mile to his hospital for work when his front wheel drive car would be thus incapacitated anyway by snowfall, also got to immerse himself in the sights, sounds and inconvenience of those rare days of heavy snowfall too. Having studied in England as well as the US too, he had had many more years to appreciate the beauty of the changing seasons. It still was no less emotive and amazing to him though.

Amidst all that though, they had to be watchful and wary of their surroundings at all times to avoid being caught up in crimes. There was that time when Gemma, waiting on a city bus at the stop with a female stranger, was accosted by a male creature who did every kind of inviting, cajoling and finally threatening to get her, 'the pretty little thing' as he'd called her to come into his car for a ride. She weighed all of one hundred and five pounds then. She then had to turn on her acting skills and tearfully tell him that she would love to go with him, but she had the 'aids' and didn't want to infect him. Once he got that message and he looked at her, really looked at her, she obviously turned from attractive meat to emaciated wench as she had intended. He burned his tires getting away from her. She had been so pitiful that the lady also waiting at the stop, started to extend condolences to her due to her purported terminal case of HIV, only to burst out laughing when Gemma explained that it was all a ruse to get rid of her suitor, more likely her near rapist/murderer. The poor lady just about rolled on the ground, barely able to contain her hilarity.

In November of 1990 roughly one year after they'd met in America, they were married in a small modest wedding on Church Avenue on a Saturday and he was back at work on that very Monday. There was just the beginning of a chill to the morning air, encouraging a light jacket with a few yellow falling leaves wafting on the breeze from the plentiful trees lining the side streets. There was a good fall season ongoing, but presumably because the cityscape was warmer and with more artificial light, the trees were still well attired with their jackets of yellow brownish leaves in Brooklyn. His half-brother from the UK and one half-sister from Canada plus a grandaunt on his side along with a few friends made it. Mom G, plus Gemma's aunt, her brother with his ex-wife Wren and a few of her friends all told less than forty folks, were there to witness the vows. There was no time nor money for a honeymoon. All funds were going to build that house in the islands. Three months later Gemma was pregnant with their first kid, a boy. Their lives continued to just bop along rapidly. Gemma had passed her big girl Nurse Certification exams and had started work as a nurse at a nursing home to 'get her feet wet' first, before tackling hospital work. That working ended with the baby coming and they spent as much time having fun as possible, when time, money and baby allowed. They both were overjoyed with each other in many ways, and particularly their seeming serendipitous reunion. It seemed amazing to Martin that he had almost given up on ever getting to really know her after years of trying from afar; to him his efforts all along had felt like paddling upstream.

Of course, there was the good, the evil and the ugly too. They were sitting in their little car one early evening at the park, with her now husband feeding their baby his bottle of milk. Interestingly, one of New York's finest supposed-to-be peace keepers, drove by then returned. There was the knock on the closed untinted window of the car and when Martin surprised, manually rolled it down said, "Hello officer, how can I help you?" The response came, "I'd like to see your ID Sir." After he went to his car and returned, handing back the papers, her husband asked why he had needed to disturb them. He was told, "It looked like you all had a can of beer drinking in the park." Supposedly, as a cop, one did not even have to make up a plausible excuse to invade and denigrate the people you viewed as lesser human beings who certainly had no right to be respected. Such was the visceral ill-feeling engendered. Neither of them were drinking nor eating except for the baby whose clear bottle filled with white milk topped by a nipple had been sitting on the car dash. They could only shake their heads in disbelief and disgust. This was their first taste of the obvious harassment that was the lot of people, particularly those of color who were trying to do the right thing peacefully. Could one even imagine being subjected to that kind of unpleasantness almost on a daily basis and the resentment it would breed.

Police forces seem to collect a much larger preponderance of bullies hiding behind a powerful badge than hopefully exist throughout the general population. The wrong antagonistic response could easily escalate into very unpleasant consequences indeed. They recognized that instances like that occurred in every country of the world, but it clarified why there was a tremendous lack of cooperation given to cops, even when it led to detrimental consequences for the neighborhood overall. The awful reality must prevail against all attempts to subvert it, was Gemma's feeling. Harassment and racism was real, to call 'a spade' just that, 'a spade'.

Finally, after almost two years of trying to arrange a return to Camerhogne and being stonewalled by the government authorities there, despite being fully qualified and board certified in Internal Medicine and board eligible in Anesthesia, her husband Martin had to pull up their fledgling roots from Brooklyn New York and haul it down to Kentucky to a 'sure job' he had committed to in June of 1993. 'A bird in the hand is better than none in the bush' he had had to finally concede. He had vowed that after more than a year of visiting the appropriate officials personally, writing the required letters of application, burning up his long-distance phone bill, he would have to commit to a job, any job by late May early June. All along he just had been amazed, confused and shocked at not having been welcomed back to his homeland with the skills and knowledge he had gone to such great lengths to accrue.

Gemma had tried her best to hint that she had seen nurses sent abroad to get special training, only to return and to have the same government not utilize them in their area of training, leading to severe frustration and them often quitting to go elsewhere. She knew the strange inexplicable schizophrenic like behavior that was rampant in their little country among the governing class. She had restrained herself so as not to highlight it too much, for fear that Martin would become convinced that she just didn't want to return there with him. Another of his former medical school colleagues who had served down there had let him know about that phenomenon too. She understood that he needed to try his best on his own, which he did. Her husband Martin, though still puzzled and disbelieving of the result obtained from his attempt to not be part of the 'brain drain', had to content himself with the knowledge that he had given it his best effort. His house had been built and they'd visited it. He had even sent down a container with tiles for the floor along with furniture. He had with help, gotten to lay down the tiles. He, they, never did get to live in it; so sad she thought. Later on, as the years passed and he was able to pay off the mortgage in Camerhogne way early, she heard him actually say, 'they did me a favor'! Yeah, things often work out for the better, just do the work and be patient.

Thus it was, that they found themselves in their little red four door sedan, in the mid-autumn month of November'93, marveling at the wonderful fall foliage in New Jersey, then Pennsylvania, on the dash through hilly Maryland and the even hillier West Virginia as they descended on the edge of southern Ohio into Kentucky. What a joy it was to take in the immense terracing along those hills to create those highways with their multicolored bare rock faces adorned with gnarled trees and shrubs at the higher elevations. The distant creeks running deep in the sometimes barely discernible valleys were part hidden by fog even late in the morning. The sudden squalls with rapidly darkening skies that would clear just around the next bend left them anticipating the very next surprise. Oh the leaves, every shade of yellow, red, orange glowing splendidly iridescent as far as the eyes could see upon arriving over some of the high mountain points during the drive. It was regrettable that they could not stop and stare at every scenic lookout that had been thoughtfully carved out at key vantage points along the highway for just that purpose. Martin though had calculated the distance and expected time of the trip. He wanted to arrive at the little town they were headed to while it was still light. They could only do the absolutely necessary stopping for gas and leg stretching. Their little two-year-old son was packed in the back center seat strapped into to his car seat and fully surrounded by their essential portable luggage. Into the bluegrass region of Kentucky crossing the Ohio river which demarcated the boundary between those two states, slipping by a roadside refinery belching stinky white smoke. The rest of the drive had been through only slightly rolling hills, in fact mostly flat compared to the prior six hours. It was beautiful, only three more hours to go. Rolling into London Kentucky they had crept into their hotel, grabbed food, then stretched out. They had flown in before for the interview in June so they already had some idea of the lay of the land. Tomorrow would begin the search for an apartment and in one week they'd be on the job, Martin at the hospital and Gemma being mommy and dear nurturing wife.

One year later Gemma's daughter came screaming out into the world. That was a year into her husband's full practice as an attending specialist in Anesthesiology and he actually got to place her labor epidural for pain relief too. She had had the luxury of an epidural for an almost pain free birth the first time around too but in good ole' Brooklyn. The baby arrived in that small hospital in rural Kentucky. Just after that milestone, there was another one; they purchased their first house in the USA. No more renting was the mantra. Once again, they threw themselves into discovery of their town and its surroundings. There were many lakes, even a State Park right there in town. The busiest National Park - the smoky mountain park was just under three hours away. So once again the two of them now accompanied by their 'little munchkins' made time for the outdoors and photography in all seasons. They could now at least comfortably afford to shoot roll after roll of film and afford to get them processed. In fact, they bought their first digital camera; just amazing to not have to go anywhere to see their pictures as it displayed on their computer screen. There was a feeling of arrival, of hope and possibilities.

Something strange had happened 'out of the blue'. It was a memory, that somehow had snuck up onto Gemma like a thief in the dark. What triggered it was hard to say. It was may be that she and her husband had been talking about their high school experiences. They had grown up in different parishes that were not adjacent either. His school though also in the country area, had figured prominently in the inter- secondary school sport competitions. His class of students also had recorded amazing results in the General Certificate Exams the year they'd taken it. He Martin her husband, had done shockingly well in the rankings overall and his results had been used by the teachers and principal of her school as a motivational whip at her school. The word was, "here is how well this little student from a poor country high school has done, so you all had better study hard to not bring shame on our school." All of a sudden Gemma remembered making the statement to her principal, "I'm going to marry that boy!" Of course, they'd all rolled their eyes and laughed saying, "You're first going to have to find a way to meet him Gemma!" All of a sudden Gemma, sitting in her own home in Kentucky realized that she had in fact, completely inexplicably, met 'that boy' and married him, all without remembering that old crazy statement of hers, which at the time was simply said for effect and fun. "Oh my God, careful what you say, careful what you wish for out loud. Your ears may hear you say it and program your brain to make it happen. Our brains are just like computers, so only speak out what you want since the ears are our keyboard," was her take home thought and ever since Gemma has lived by that edict.

Being comfortably ensconced in a small rural town in Kentucky brought the opportunity for lots of mental reflection that would have been harder to do while still living amidst the daily grind in New York City. She now lived in a small town of five thousand people. Just Laurel county her new place of abode, was more than twice the square mileage of the whole nation of Camerhogne, yet had less than half the population of her island nation and in that way too, it was the polar opposite to New York City. It blew her mind to think that there were one hundred twenty total number of such counties just in the relatively rural state of Kentucky alone and there were forty nine other states! On the other hand the population in her Laurel county would have occupied just a few blocks of territory in New York City, with people living like rats one on top of the other. Even the mongooses in their cliff hole dens behind her old home in Zion were not so crowded she wagered. So good to be out of the great New York City she thought, tempering that thought a bit, in the knowledge that her mom G still lived there. Her mom G though could not be dragged away even in chains from her community of friends and her church family. So many folks had migrated from Camerhogne and they had rebuilt their community in New York City, settling mostly within the borough of Brooklyn. So there was a built-in community there for her, especially in her age group. The younger more professional generations who were on their way up the ladder were dispersing to Atlanta, Texas and Florida mostly. When she spoke to those types, they usually asked her, "You moved to where, Kentucky?"

There in New York City, she had left the ultra rich, both old money and the newly rich plus the craven politicians who they supported and who in turn catered to their needs. These were the ones who alternated between their homes in the Hamptons and their office towers in Manhattan, when they were not in their private jets. Gemma grinned to herself at the thought that she had never knowingly met any of those people personally and likely never would. There was the upper middle class 'peacock proud' of their nice brownstones and their Bahamas vacations, the larger 'middling' middle class proud of their nice little Nissan maximas and the even larger 'lower' middle class, followed by the masses of poor people who just eked out a living, with the desperate miserable poorest of the poor 'scrounging' along day by day. Further down the totem pole were the famous New York City rats. They were remarkably large, bold, resilient and world famous. She did not miss any of them at all. People were the same all over, just like the class structure at her home nation starting with the hoity-toity of Camerhogne, to its smaller middle class on down to the home challenged.

Thus those poor mostly people of color, found it hard to push their kids into college which was the way out of poverty ultimately. That college thing had been the ticket out, for her and Martin. It had been the way forward for all the other ethnic groups out there too. Black folks couldn't hide their blackness as could the Irish, Italians and Jews who just melded and blended into the rest of society starting from the first generation if they tried. Those other groups simply lost their accents, got educated and moved on and often out. Non-white folks were forever the target of discrimination for that black skin, Lordy. Thus, even when a few of their kids 'broke through the ceiling' they faced official and unofficial discrimination to get an equal shake at that job at the appropriate level. That wasn't helped when they were being dragged down to the bottom of the barrel by their own black neighborhood through balkanized speech patterns that further marginalized them, the drug culture and the black on black crime. This was the true 'crabs in a barrel effect', where any crab making progress climbing out of the barrel, got dragged back down into it. Remarkably, the sons of the former white immigrants, got hired at quite good salaries to come back from the suburbs to over-police those same 'black high crime' neighborhoods.

Overall though, her take on the state of the whole of America's evolution was that despite all its much touted constitution, rule of law, attempt to prevent the tyranny of one man rule, stated attempt to create a home for the disaffected, the unstated part was that it was for male people who look a certain caucasoid way. They were the ones being catered to and who therefore managed to gain monetary, political and societal prominence. Once they got that, they hung on tooth and nail, to keep that power. Gemma could see the parallels to the society in Camerhogne and it remained starkly clear that human nature flowed fluidly across cultures and nations. In that way, these United States had not progressed much beyond the Romans who conquered many lands over centuries, demonstrated unimaginable technology to span rivers, create major roads, construct temporarily impregnable forts and cities, all the while riding on the backs of slaves and a massive underclass. If America had truly emancipated its 'other', encouraged growth for all, can anyone imagine the immense talents, dormant, hidden, suppressed, that could have been released to further catapult this nation beyond the reach of more seemingly homogeneous autocratic societies out east she wondered.

Every now and again, against great odds, flashes of such entrepreneurial or inventive greatness appear often from among the much maligned immigrants, the striving middle class, and not usually from the fat and happy multi-generation citizens who just seek to maintain their blue-blood rich status quo. Can man be more sensible, more magnanimous, smarter than his blueprint? Gemma had to admit that from her reading, observing, and limited experience, no other place seemed so well positioned, based on political framework at least, to give everyone who worked for it, a fairer shake. That was the promise, the greatness of America and on a smaller scale New York City, but it was a constant struggle with only a few flashes of breakthrough success. Coming from the village of Zion, where the frogs mashed and agitated their watery environment to keep their eggs aerated, it was all clear to her; the unending struggle of life continues, just as it always had in prior civilizations including the more well known like those of the Greeks and the Romans. There was mashing, thrashing around, frothing, and constant struggle among the masses of the lower class and underclasses in New York City, with only the lucky few emerging relatively unscathed. The big apple was a place for big struggle.

Sitting on her new couch, her kids taking a nap, Gemma leaned back and allowed herself to think of the New York they'd just left, having spent four years in its bowels. A smile passed over her face as she remembered two funny incidents that helped her to get her 'sea-legs', as sailors would say. She had seen this young-man begging near the entrance to the underground train called the subway, and naively had made eye contact at which point he had made his pitch, sunk in his hook and pulled the line taut. Fresh from Camerhogne, heart on her sleeve, she had dug into her pocket and handed the man her bus fare that was to get her back to Wren's apartment some twelve long blocks away. That would have been a long walk. Instead the beggar said, "Who do you think I am, a child? You give me a bunch of coins!" He threw it all back on her, and she scrambled to pick it all up and return them to her pocket. No good deed goes unpunished! She was red around the ears, not in shame, but with intense anger at being so fooled by that scamp! After that experience, now wiser, she observed one such beggar leaving his post, step behind a parked vehicle and quickly slip off his 'stage gear'. All of the old shaggy dirty looking clothing went into a bag, and he stepped out with sharp looking blue jeans, neat jacket and now in sharp leather shoes. At a distance she took a chance and followed him as he made his way to a new looking higher-end German built automobile. It was all she could do to not fall on her face with laughter then, at the audacity of that scam artist. New York, New York, home of the best street actors playing the role of beggar. She never ever again even looked in the direction of anyone who looked like they were trying to make eye contact while there. None of her hard earned money was to go to 'beggars'.

Initially, when she had just arrived in the city, every block pretty much resembled each other. After weeks and months though, the differences between blocks, then between neighborhoods, became clearer. She began to appreciate the differences and the beauty of each. One could walk or drive through and see the stark differences in upkeep, adornment and gentrification that told stories about which neighborhoods were owner occupied versus mostly rentals. Even by listening to the music on street corners and viewing the types of storefronts plus observing the garb of the folks walking by, would inform one of what kind of folks lived there. Some streets were amazing to walk or drive though, with so many different garbs displayed, from the ultra orthodox Jewish men with their tallit, heavy black garb of the Hasidic with their furry black hats and facial hair, to the sari-clad folks from India, shalwar kameez and kurta of the Pakistanis, alongside miniskirt-clad youngsters with multicolored hair. Gemma couldn't help but think of tropical birds in a zoo.

There was the fantastic glitz of various Manhattan districts that came to mind whenever people thought of New York City and America really. The Times Square, Theater district, Macy's store, the storied history of Harlem in its heyday with its music and dancing inventiveness, its sky scrapers, Empire State Building, the World Trade Centers, man-made Central Park and so many other firsts in the world. There unfortunately, was also the dirty underbelly of New York City, as folks referred to it. She had arrived at a time when the AIDS epidemic was booming in New York City with people dying like flies and early treatment regimens were almost as toxic as the disease. It almost felt like she was being chased from Camerhogne by it, since she had become aware of its existence even back there. The crack cocaine boom was taking a toll on families and society, along with the harsh law-enforcement that accompanied it.

Furthermore all of those population groups in NYC interestingly, had their criminal cabals similar to the Italian mob who prey on their own, as well as any and all within their reach. Many progressive middle class Caribbean folks couldn't wait to get out of New York City, to be able to provide their children a safer, better upbringing, with better educational options than typically within reach of their income if they continued to live in the city. Gemma and her husband belonged to that latter group who had wanted out, she concluded. She was convinced that they'd done the right thing.

In her new rural environment, people by and large were pleasant and respectful; it was a breath of fresh air to find that place. Yes, she was initially scared on her first visit with her husband for the interview. Right there in the hospital parking lot, a burly gruff looking individual drove up and parked next to their rented car with his battered green pickup truck with a long gun splayed across its back window seeming inches from the back of his head. She sank down in her seat to appear to be as small as possible. Her husband had already climbed up the steps of the mobile home that served as the office of the CEO at the time, while his office was undergoing renovations. She was shocked when people actually noticed her existence and said a pleasant, "Hello ma'am, how are you?" These were perfect strangers too. That would never happen in New York City, where one was as transparent as glass. People looked straight through you. If they did actually look at you, as did beggars and con-artists, beware you were their target! She had had to learn the sophisticated big city stare, eyes wide open making sure to see everything around you, particularly those things that might threaten one's survival while not focusing on anyone. Here in rural Kentucky, people stared hard at you, directly in the eyes, expecting acknowledgement oftentimes. Ah, that demanded resurrecting the interpersonal skills more suited to her old life in Camerhogne.

From the frying pan, into the fire. Again, human nature was under scrutiny. Church called and she answered. Her little family went to church and it was amazing how friendly people were, particularly once they discovered that her husband Martin was now one of their local specialist physicians. The lists came out, giving the percentage of his salary that was to be given in tithes, the other percentage for the building fund and the various committee assignments that were to be had. That had not happened in New York City despite the many years of church attendance there, so it was rather striking and even shocking in its lack of tact. This was one the first visit; hey buddy, here's the price of admission! These people obviously took their religion way seriously. Gemma's tradition back in Camerhogne was to be well dressed for church and so was more than a bit taken aback by the totally casual dress code exhibited by most of the congregation. Then the nice lady who she happened to sit by in the pew, took one look at her and grabbed her scruffy bag violently away from between her and Gemma, placing it on her other side. She sidled her rear away too as far as she possibly could and not in a nice way. Gemma realized that she was being treated as a contagion. It was as if the poor lady felt she had something that Gemma would want; in fact Gemma's purse and clothing were visibly far more expensive. Being in the house of the Lord, meant that Gemma chose to ignore the poor lady rather than give her the 'death stare'! Church didn't seem like such a good idea after all. The unvarnished grasping was a huge turnoff; you may not be all that welcome, just send the money. Obviously some people had their prejudices and this was the South, as she had been warned over and over!

As she walked her new baby girl in arms in the little paved driveway, older son also in tow, Gemma lost herself in the mass of gladiolas, forget me nots, hydrangeas, boxwoods, hostas, russian sage flourishing in the chipped wood covered beds around her enclosed double car garage door. She felt at peace. Even amidst the peace, there was disquiet too though. She had to remind herself to be very careful when tending the garden, since she had found a few shed snakeskins in that very same garden in early summer. There were no yellow serpents hanging from the rafters over her bed, but she did need to be careful of their brothers and sister rattlesnakes that might lurk within her flower beds. They had thoughtfully left evidence of their presence in the garden that she took as a kindly warning. Certain things remained constant though. Wherever she went though, Gemma did what she liked best, growing things.

THE END.

Blurb 1:
An unusually gutsy ten-year-old growing up in the rural northern side of an idyllic island nation navigating all the twists and traps of village life. Those traps that would doom her chance of a good future are set all around her by mostly respectable seeming adults. Can she adroitly step through that social minefield and emerge unscathed?

Summary:
Join Gemma coming from a rural island nation, and a poor though not impoverished, family background with both the benefit and dangers of a wealthy family as her closest neighbor. She works hard to avoid the pitfalls everywhere around her, any of which would doom any reasonable chance of an upstanding future adult life. Guided by luck and her own inner compass, we gain insight into her sometimes stumbling progress out of those circumstances.

Blurb 2:
A gritty tale reflecting the realities of village life facing an ordinary yet resourceful young ten year old girl growing up in the beautiful tropical island nation of Camerhogne. Can she beat the odds to become an accomplished educated productive young lady?

AUTHORS : D. Gemcats Purcell and Catherine G Purcell married spouses for over thirty years, live in the USA but are originally from the Caribbean